Hagar, Mother of Sorrows

Angelique Conger

Copyright

Table of Contents

To the women who think they get seconds,

and find it becomes the best.

To the women who think they get seconds,
and find it becomes the best.

Well

C rocodiles shaped my life. I hate crocodiles, but my earliest memories are of crocodiles on the river. Some call our river the Nile, but we of Egypt call it the Aur, or the Black River, because in times of flood, it filled the valley with life-giving soil. This soil helped our fields grow more grains than any other land we knew.

When I was less than three years old, Father and Mother took my brother Nesu and me to the riverbank. Mother took a basket full of food. I remember the bright blue cloth she brought from the basket to lay our food on.

I played next to the river close to my family, digging in the sand. I remember a gray-green log floated to the shore. Curious, I toddled toward it.

Mother screamed behind me.

Something strange happened. The log opened up. Big teeth filled the insides.

Father snatched me up and ran away as the jaws slammed shut on the empty air where I had stood. Nesu told me later a crocodile almost got me that day.

Mother screamed again and called me her baby, then berated me as she scrambled to gather our lunch up and hurried toward home.

Mother never went with the family to the river again, and kept me home as long as she could. She was terrified of the crocodiles.

Father had brought Mother to a small home near the river when they married. Together, they farmed a small plot of land that fed and provided them with enough extra to trade for other necessities.

Life was tough for them, but my brother and I knew our parents loved us. We never felt less than the others in our part of Memphis, probably because we all lived in the same conditions.

Mother panicked when a neighbor child younger than me went missing. The child had strayed too close to the river and a crocodile ate it.

Mother pulled Nesu and I close to her and wailed.

"Never go close to the river. Do you understand, Nesu?"

Nesu nodded. "Yes, Mother."

"And you, Hagar. Do you understand you must stay away from the crocodiles?"

Tears filled my eyes at the loss of my little playmate, and because Mother was so upset. "Yes, Mother. I will stay away from those mean crocodiles."

Nesu secretly took me to the river as we grew older, however. He would always remind me to watch for the floating logs. "You never know which ones will be crocodiles," he would warn.

Mother asked us if we went near the river when we returned, but we always told her we had stayed far away. She did not need to know.

Memphis was a big city, built by those who discovered Egypt long ago. Father told me our ancestor, Egyptus, had brought her family here before the tower at Babel and the language changes. He said we speak the language of the Fathers. I doubted it, for I have seen our language change in the years I have lived.

Mother sent me to the well for water when I grew big enough to carry an urn. We did not drink from the Aur, for the dirt and silt in it made it undrinkable. Sadly for me, I was not tall then like I am now. Boys in our part of town thought it funny to push me over and spill my water. Sometimes I had to dip water five times before they allowed me to pass and take the water back to Mother.

I refused to complain or cry. I had watched other girls cry, and the boys never stopped bullying them. When they pushed me over, I would retrieve my urn and return to wait my turn at the well.

One day, Nesu saw the boys push me over.

"Why have you not told me about this?" he asked as he joined me at the well. "Mother sent me to find you since you have been gone so long. She thinks you have been playing near the well, rather than getting her water."

"I would never do that," I cried. "Those bullies think it is funny to watch a girl trudge back and forth to get water and never get it home to their Mother." I poured more water into my urn.

"And you never told me? Why?" Nesu helped balance the urn on my shoulder.

I frowned and lifted my free shoulder. "It is my problem. If I cry, they will never stop bullying." I walked away from the well toward the boys.

Nesu padded beside me. "There are other ways to get past them. You need not walk past them every time."

"That is the way home," I pointed out. "To go another way would take longer."

"And returning for water takes less time?" Nesu asked.

We neared the boys and Nesu glared at them. "Leave my sister alone."

The boys jeered and taunted him, but they did not push me over. Relieved, I took the water to my mother.

After that, I turned away from them, walking a longer path to return to our home. Sometimes Nesu would come with me to warn away the bullies when Mother needed the water quickly.

In the weeks after I began walking along the longer path, I watched the boys who loved to persecute us while waiting for my turn at the well. Girls had banded together, waiting for each other to walk past them in groups. It became more difficult to cause problems with them.

3

Sometimes, the girl on the outside edge would have her water pushed off her shoulder, but the girls chastised the boys intensely.

On the days Nesu could not accompany me to the well, I waited for my friends to fill their urns and walked with them a longer way. It became a pleasant time for me to go to the well, for I could visit with friends and walk home with them. I enjoyed this time with them.

When Mother asked about the time it took, I told her we waited for each other to avoid the bully boys. With nostrils flaring and breathing heavily, she wanted to rush to the well and berate them.

"No, Mother," I cried, stopping her at the door. "We have it under control. The boys have not disturbed our water collection for more than a week. Now they stand and make ugly sounds as we pass by them."

"Because you are beautiful girls," Mother said. "But I need the water faster. Is there another way you can hurry?"

"I will try, Mother."

I really tried to get the water and return home faster, but it was not as easy as she thought it would be. I still had to wait for the other girls or walk the long way. Neither would take me home any faster.

Mother finally sighed and reconciled herself to a longer wait. Sometimes she sent me earlier, if she needed water faster. But she never went to the well for herself.

"Hagar, you must be careful today," Nesu said as I lifted my empty urn to my shoulder.

"Why? Those boys gave up pushing the water from our shoulders years ago." I gave an impatient huff. My friends waited for me.

"Can you mess up your hair, put mud on your face? Something to make you less beautiful?" His insistence puzzled me.

"Why should I?"

"Pharaoh's men are searching through the city for women to take to the palace."

"Why would that be terrible?" I rocked on my feet, eager to leave for the well.

"Women disappear inside the palace and never return. I am not ready to lose you to the men of the palace yet."

I thought of Bau, the boy who hung around the well, wanting to carry my water with a little blush. I would not want to appear looking ugly, neither did I desire to be taken by Pharaoh's men. I shuddered at the thought. I had heard stories of young women going missing and never seen on the streets again.

I flinched again as Nesu mussed my hair and painted mud on my face. I did not like to look untidy and ugly.

"Slump your shoulders," Nesu suggested.

"Do you really believe I have to worry? I am young, barely a woman."

"Old enough for the men of the palace to want to have their way with you," Nesu warned.

I slumped.

"Can you limp?"

I nodded and set the urn on my shoulder. It was difficult to carry it slumping and limping. "This is hard," I whined.

"It will be harder for you if Pharaoh's men take you," Nesu growled. "I will walk with you some of the way, but Father needs me in the fields."

"Go to the fields with Father," I said. "I will do as you say. With this mud on my face, no one will think of me as a beauty."

"Do not depend on the mud. Even I can see you are beautiful through the mud. Be sure to limp and slump. Let your mouth fall slack."

"Like the girl who is mad?"

5

She came to the well sometimes while the other girls were there. Some girls said cruel and unkind things to her. I tried to befriend her, remembering how it felt to have the boys be so unkind. She would have nothing to do with me and backed away when I tried to approach her. It saddened me.

"Yes, like her. Pharaoh's men will not take her."

I let my mouth sag. "Like this?"

"Yes," Nesu said. "Can you drool a bit as well?"

"Drool? I am not a child." I wrinkled my nose.

"But it will save you."

I shook my head. "You are certain?"

"I am not certain of anything when I think of Pharaoh's men taking our women. I only know I do not want them to take you from us."

I set my urn on the ground and embraced my brother. "Thank you for caring."

"I must go help Father. He will not be happy with me for leaving him alone in the field for so long. But I had to warn you. Be careful."

I watched Nesu trot down the path toward our field. Father had not eaten or slept well in the last few days. He snapped at us at the smallest provocation. I heard him moan when he thought no one was near. Something was happening. I had become cautious in his presence as concern wrapped my gut. I hoped Nesu and Father would have a decent harvest.

I lifted my urn back to my shoulder and remembered to slump. That meant I had to use a hand to steady the urn. When I stretched tall, it balanced with ease on my shoulder.

I limped, slumped, and let my mouth hang slack, struggling to walk down the path toward the well. I hoped the other girls had brothers or fathers to warn them.

When I finally arrived at the well, the others were just leaving.

"Why are you so slow?" Mehi asked. "And why the mud?"

"Did you not hear? Pharaoh's men are searching for women."

6

"Not again," Sitra cried.

"They were here yesterday after you left," Mehi said, glancing about the square.

The girls scattered toward home, turning this way and that like a flock of birds, avoiding a net. Only Nena stayed near the well.

"There they are," Nena yelped. "How do I avoid them?"

Big men dressed in Pharaoh's colors marched into the square in a tight squad. They frowned and turned toward us.

Nena shrunk behind the well, trying to hide from them.

"Slump. Limp. Muss you hair," I squeaked through a dry throat.

I limped to the well and dropped the bucket down. With shaky hands I pulled it up as the pounding of feet warned me Pharaoh's men were close, filling the space near the well.

"We seek beautiful women for the palace," the leader announced. "Turn so we can see you."

I kept pulling on the rope. *Would the mud and my slobber be enough to protect me from these men? What would Mother do if they take me?*

"All of you," he snapped.

Were there others here? I thought they had all run.

I slowly turned and flinched when I saw Sitra standing among them with her lips trembling, held by one of the men. I shook my head slightly, not wanting their attention on me. I let my mouth sag and drool slid past my lips. Normally, I would be aghast, but today I allowed it.

I clutched my urn to my chest and gawked at the leader's feet. I hoped to look smaller.

My gaze darted to the right and the left. Other young women I did not know fidgeted with their dresses, tears streaming down their faces, with lips mumbling prayers.

I would consider praying, but I did not trust Elkenah and would not pray to Sobek, the crocodile god. I shuddered at the thought. Not after my close encounter with a crocodile as a child.

The leader walked along the line of young women. When he got to me, he lifted my chin with his leather wrapped whip.

My eyes bulged and I moaned. I allowed more drool to slide from my mouth onto his whip.

He pulled it back with a curse, setting me off balance so I struggled to stand erect, and stomped to the next young woman, wiping my drool from his hand.

He took three more young women I did not know. I was among those left behind. I sighed as they tromped away.

The other girls hugged and jumped together as they celebrated their freedom.

"Why did they not take me?" Nena complained. "I am more beautiful than Sitra."

"Be grateful they passed you by," I said. "You do not know what happens to those who disappear within the walls of the palace."

"Their mothers can no longer force them to get water," Nena grumbled.

"Are you certain? I would rather get my mother water than face the unknown of the palace. I fear what they would do to me there." I clutched my urn to my chest and limped away.

"Why do you continue to pretend you are ugly?" Nena asked, walking beside me. "Pharaoh's men are gone."

"They may have moved on, but I do not trust them."

My hip hurt from limping when I finally opened the door to our home.

Mother looked up from her cleaning and glared at me. "Why are you covered in mud? You know better than to go out looking like that," she growled.

"Pharaoh's men were searching for young women to take to the palace." I set the urn on the floor and rubbed my hip. "Nesu insisted I look ugly. He painted me with this mud."

"And they left you alone?" she asked, moving in closer and touching the mud on my face.

I closed my eyes and huffed out my breath through my nose. "They took Sitra and three others. I drooled on the leader's hand. He would have nothing to do with me."

Mother gasped, then grinned at me. "Smart girl. What would I do if they took you?"

Many times after that I saw Pharaoh's men tramping through the city, searching for young women to take to the palace.. I would immediately begin slumping, limping, and drooling. For a time, it worked.

Sorrow

F ather finally admitted to his concerns one evening after the fall harvest. "The price of grains has dropped. I did not harvest enough grain from our small farm to bring enough coins for us to live on for the next year. I do not know how we will live."

"We will find a way," Mother said. "I can make baskets and sheets of papyrus to sell. I have seen papyrus used as sails on boats that ply up and down the Aur."

"I provide for my family," Father growled. But he dropped his head into his hands. "But with the price of grain dropping, I do not see how I can continue to farm."

I stared at my beloved father. *He could do anything. I had seen it. He often told us we could do anything we wanted if we tried hard enough.* Yet, now he sat with his head in his hands, dejected.

Although I had grown too big to sit on his lap months earlier, I crawled into his lap and draped my arms across his neck. "You can do this, Father," I whispered.

His arms surrounded me as he sobbed into my shoulder. "I do not know how."

I peered up at Mother, searching for answers. Her face had crumpled like Father's. She leapt to her feet and walked with jerky steps to the table and poured herself a cup of wine.

Nesu shook his head. His gaze dropped to the ground.

"What will we do?" Father moaned. "If I do not have enough coins, the tax collector will take our home. Where would we live then?" He rocked back and forth, clutching me in his arms. I stared at Nesu in fear.

"Perhaps," Nesu rasped. He cleared his throat and tried again. "Perhaps we can do something else?"

Father glared at Nesu, then leaned forward. I feared he would hit my brother, so I clung to his neck. Father slumped back in his seat.

"What could we do? Are you old enough and big enough to do the work of a man?" Father sneered.

Mother and I lifted our eyebrows and grimaced.

"Perhaps not old enough." Nesu's jaw jutted out imperceptibly. "But I have worked beside you for the last three years. I can do the work of a man."

"Not enough to save us," Father said, shoving me off his lap and standing.

I stumbled into the corner and huddled there, watching the men I loved.

Nesu held firm with his fists clenched by his side. "It was not my fault, or yours, that the buyers have reduced the price they pay for grain. We can eat our grain if they will not buy it."

Father took a threatening step toward Nesu.

"Father, no!" I cried.

He turned and swung his fist in my direction. I ducked and stepped back enough to avoid his fist, shocked that he would consider hitting Nesu or me.

"This is between me and your brother," he growled.

I dared not say anything else and returned to the corner of the small room. Mother tipped her glass back and drained her wine. The evening became stranger by the moment.

"How will we pay the taxes on our land if we eat our grain? How will we pay the taxes on our home? Pharaoh demands payment ."

"We can do something else, perhaps farm ..."

"Farming takes all the hours of the day if we are to have enough to keep us alive," Father roared. "How can we farm and do something else?"

He glared at Nesu for many long moments before plopping back into his chair and grabbing and pulling fists full of his hair.

Nesu swallowed thickly. "I heard Tebu lost his helpers ..."

"Tebu?" Father asked.

"The boatman. He hauls grain and other things up and down the Aur in his boat. Oba and Ti left him, thinking they could do better," Nesu rubbed the back of his neck. "We can ask him for the job."

"You would have me work for another? A boatman?" Father snorted.

"It would pay. I have heard Tebu say he needs help."

"And what makes you think he would hire me? What's more, what makes you think he will hire you? You are but a boy." Father wrinkled his nose.

Nesu bit his lower lip. "Because I spoke to him today. He says we can begin in the morning."

"But you cannot swim," Mother blurted from the corner where she cowered.

"I do not need to swim," Nesu said. "I need to stand on the boat. I need to unload the cargo. Why should I swim?"

"What if you fall in?" I asked under my breath.

Nesu turned to me. "I will grab onto the edge of the boat and pull myself in. Besides," he turned to Mother, "I can swim. I taught myself to swim when I was little."

Mother squeezed her eyes shut.

"I knew you could swim," Father said. "I have seen you in the river with the other boys. But that did not give you the right to talk to Tebu for me." He spoke through clenched teeth.

"I did not agree that you would join Tebu in the morning. I only said I would be there, and perhaps my father would join me."

"What gave you the right to share our problems with others?" Father growled, jumping from his chair and advancing toward Nesu.

Nesu did not move. "I said nothing about our problems. Everyone knows the price of grain is down. Tebu came to me, asking if I knew anyone who could help him. There is much grain to transport this year, and he needs help."

"So you thought you would leave me and go help Tebu?"

"We harvested all our grain. I can work for Tebu during the day and help you in the evening."

"There will be nothing to help with," Father said, deflating like the stomach of a pig. "I sold the farm today. It is Heru's problem now."

My breath caught.

"You sold the farm?" Mother rushed from her corner to confront Father. "How could you do that without talking to me about it? Where will we live?"

"Heru spoke with me about it last week. Today he brought me a bag of coins. He does not want our hovel." Father peered at our small home and huffed. "Just our farm. You know he tries every year to purchase it from me to expand his land.".

Mother dropped into her chair and rocked back and forth. "What will we do?" she moaned.

What will we do? How can I help?

"You will do as you suggested. You will gather the papyrus reeds and make sheets of papyrus to sell at the market," Father said with a growl. "We will need more than Nesu and I will make working on Tebu's barge."

"I can help with that," I said. "I can cut papyrus reeds."

"You will stay away from the river," Mother snapped. "I will not lose you to a crocodile."

"A crocodile will not eat me. I know how to watch for crocodiles. I am old enough to know how to be safe near the river," I argued. "You will need me to help watch for the crocodiles and carry the loads of reeds if we are to make enough papyrus to sell."

"But — but ..." Mother stuttered.

"Hagar is right," Father said. "If you are to make enough papyrus to sell, you will need her help."

He stalked over to take Nesu's hand. "What time do we begin?"

"At sunrise."

It was not unusual for our family to rise before dawn. Farmers rose early to be on the land in the cool of the morning. But this morning we were awake and up earlier than that. My fear of the unknown had wormed its way into my stomach.

I had spoken bravely to my mother the night before, but crocodiles crowded my dreams, all with wide mouths, waiting to eat me.

Mother prepared food for us to eat and some to take with us for later, but my stomach roiled and I could not eat. She looked at me and lowered her eyebrows, although she said nothing to me.

We bid Father and Nesu goodbye near the Aur and walked in opposite directions. They turned south while we moved north toward the papyrus islands.

As we neared the water, I searched the shore and the water for crocodiles, especially for the log-like shapes of the hungry animals hiding in the water. Mother's eyes flicked up and down the riverbank as her feet dragged through the sand.

I hurried to walk beside her. We both carried large baskets with our knives in our belts. I kept my hand near my knife, ready to protect us from a crocodile.

After ensuring no crocodiles hid nearby, we set our baskets on the ground at a large island of papyrus. Mother swiftly cut the papyrus while I carried it to the baskets. Within an hour, we had more than we could carry in our baskets, all the time watching for the crocodiles grunting and growling from the surrounding river. Mother and I lifted our baskets and hurried toward home.

As we left the river bank, a low growl chilled my blood. A crocodile. Mother pushed me. "Run!"

We ran away from the riverbank as fast as we could and still hold on to all our papyrus. I heard the lumbering of a crocodile behind us and ran faster.

When at last we could no longer hear the crocodile behind us, we stopped and dropped our baskets. I placed my hands on my knees, gulping in huge breaths, trying to refill my lungs. Papyrus reeds scattered on the surrounding ground, but we did not care.

The crocodile roared, and I looked back to see it waddling back into the water. He could have eaten me in one bite!

Mother squealed and ran a few steps away.

"He is in the water now," I soothed. "We can gather up our papyrus before we go home."

I noticed a scattered path of papyrus between the river and us. Did I dare go back for it?

"We worked too hard for this papyrus," I muttered. "I am going back for all those reeds we dropped."

"But the crocodile," Mother yelped.

"Tell me if he comes out of the river." I marched back toward the river, my eyes sweeping back and forth along the riverbank, searching for crocodiles. Near the river, I bent and gathered the papyrus reeds we had dropped. As I gathered the reeds, I backed toward Mother, always watching for a crocodile to lumber from the water in my direction. I knew how fast they could travel. It would be difficult to outrun one if I had a late start.

Mother gasped as I neared her. "That big one is looking this way."

"We must look tasty to him." My macabre joke did not make her laugh.

I dumped the papyrus reeds into our baskets and grabbed mine up. "We should go."

Mother lifted her basket into her arms and tramped past me, faster than she usually walked. I had to hurry to keep up.

At home, we dumped the papyrus into a great pile before we went inside to get water. When we returned to our pile, it had grown and now other women squatted around the pile.

"We see you are going to sell papyrus sheets or woven baskets," Tali said, pulling her long, dark hair back behind her. "Your escape from the crocodile frightened me, and I watched from far away. My son gathers papyrus for me."

"And you put yours with mine?" Mother asked.

"We all did," Tali said, gesturing to the other three women. "We thought many hands would lighten the load."

"Why would you do that?" Mother bent her head to the side, not understanding.

We could make more sheets of papyrus with all this, but we would also share the income from it. Would it be enough to supplement Father's and Nesu's work on the boat?

"We saw Heru on your land late last night, striding through the fields as if he owned it," Samira growled. Her green eyes glinted in the sunshine.

"He does," Mother groaned, pushing a stray strand of her dark hair behind her ear.

"As we suspected when we saw you and Hagar walking toward the river with your men this morning," Nubit said. Tall and slender, she had folded herself to sit next to the pile of papyrus.

Mother was a private woman, at least she was when I knew her last. She harrumphed. "So?"

"So we decided you must need some help. Besides, we could all use extra coins. Many hands make the job easier," Anta replied from beneath her straw hat that protected her pale face.

"And share in the coins?" Mother crossed her arms.

As I wondered. What will they say?

"What did you plan to do with your papyrus?" Tali asked.

"Sheets of papyrus, large ones. The river men are using papyrus for sails. Thought we would get more coins for the larger sheets," Mother said, rolling her lips inward.

"Oh, I like that idea," Anta said, her voice bright.

"If we all work together, we can make it bigger," Tali suggested. "And we can use the outer portions of the reeds to make baskets and other things to sell."

I remained still beside my mother, waiting to see how she would accept this invasion of her privacy. Her head wobbled back and forth and she ran her hands through her hair.

"Can your sons help get the reeds or protect us from the crocodiles while we gather them?" She huffed out a breath. "Those creatures scare me."

"Me, too," the other women chorused.

"If there are more of us out there gathering the reeds, we can have someone watching while the rest of us gather. We can get more each time," Nubit said. "My son is good with his bow. He will go with us."

"And my son is good with his spear," Anta added.

"I cannot ask Nesu to help," Mother said. "He and Erfan work now for Tebu on his barge."

"Your family must take care of its needs. We understand," Tali said, sharing a comforting look with Mother. "Heru may take our land next. We must all be prepared."

Mother ducked her head. Tali was right. Although we should have seen it coming, we had not. Tali and the others would be better prepared.

I took my knife and cut off the dark green outer parts of the papyrus reeds. The women sitting around the pile of papyrus did the same, quickly cutting away the thick, heavy greenery. We sliced the light green center into thin strips and dropped them in the tall, broad urn I brought from the house.

The women stayed, chattering with Mother and slicing up the papyrus. When the centers were all soaking in tall, broad urns, we took the outer dark green strips and wove them into baskets, fishing pots, hats, and other useful items. Mother and I had woven papyrus for our home for years, although we had not done it for sale before.

"We can take these to the market in the morning," Tali said. "And the next day, return to the river for more papyrus."

The women agreed. We would work together and make coins to help all our families.

Mother and I worked together with our friends for more than a year, weaving objects from the outer, dark green part of the papyrus plant and making large sheets of the thin papyrus used both by sail makers and scribes. Our papyrus sheets were the finest quality, and they paid us the highest prices for them.

With our share of the coins, Mother and I purchased many of our needs. Nesu and Father no longer needed to work so hard on the barge. However, the men enjoyed the work and were working to save enough coins to purchase a barge of their own.

One day, we tromped out to the river with the other women to cut more papyrus. The sons of Nubit and Anta, boys who were becoming men, traveled with us each week to guard us as we cut and carried our gigantic baskets full of the papyrus reed back to our home.

Tebu's barge, made of papyrus and loaded with an enormous pile of grain, floated near us as I cut papyrus. I glanced up to watch my brother float past as I often did. I wanted to wave, but knew it would embarrass him.

Tebu's little daughter walked along the top of the grain that day. Her white shift stood out against the golden grain and the blue of the sky. She seldom joined her father on the barge, but she had ridden on top of the grain often enough that she was stable and her footing was sure.

The barge jolted suddenly. It must have hit something, probably the huge grandfather crocodile that liked to roam in that part of the Aur River. Tebu shouted out as his little daughter lost her balance and tumbled down the hill of grain. She screamed and scrabbled to maintain her balance.

Nesu raced to stop her, but she tumbled into the water. My heart pounded and my breath caught as he did not hesitate, leaping into the water after the little girl. He swam out to her and pulled her close.

My habit of watching for crocodiles did not stop as I watched Nesu pull Tebu's little daughter to the barge. Grandfather Crocodile emerged from behind the boat.

I gasped. Intent on the two in the water, he swam toward them. I put my fist in my mouth, fearing a scream would frighten mother. But she and the other women saw the crocodile as well, for they all shouted to Nesu to get out of the water.

I ran to the edge of the river, screaming at him. "Out of the water. The crocodile!"

Mother and the other women joined me, calling to him, trying to get his attention. My heart pounded in my ears as I screamed at Nesu, begging him to climb into the barge. My jaw hurt from clenching between my screams.

Perhaps he did not understand our words. He confidently handed the girl up to Father, then waved at us. I wanted to swim out to him and shake him. "Can you not see Grandfather Crocodile coming your way?"

I spun around, searching for a rock to throw at the beast. There were none.

Suddenly, Father saw the crocodile and shouted, pointing behind Nesu. From a distance, I could not see Father clearly, but his fear was unmistakable.

Time stands still in my memory. Nesu reached for the edge of the barge to pull himself out of the water. The enormous crocodile swam closer to him, catching him by the waist. Nesu hit at the crocodile's head with his fists, trying to make him let go.

Father and Tebu grabbed the long poles they used to pole the barge up and down the river and beat at the crocodile, but he would not let go.

Nesu's scream still haunts me. We women on the riverbank howled. I closed my eyes, not wanting to see, but could not avoid it. I opened them, willing the crocodile to open his gigantic jaws.

Nesu's wail stopped sharply. The silence was unbearable after the cries.

Father gently pulled what was left of Nesu onto the boat.

Mother's shriek would have sent fear into the hearts of the ancestors. With tears drenching their faces, Nubit and Samira took her by the hands and led her home, sobbing. Anta and Tali, who also shed many tears of horror and sadness, led me home. My pain-filled wails echoed Mother's shrieks.

My brother, my kind, helpful protector was gone into the belly of the gigantic grandfather crocodile.

I huddled on my bed, staring at nothing until Father brought what was left of Nesu's body home to prepare it for burial. Mother whimpered as she rocked in her chair. At Father's urgent call, I dragged myself off the bed.

"I must speak to the priests about his burial. Stay here with him. Keep your mother away."

I nodded dumbly. What was I to do? I avoided looking at my brother's broken body. I wanted to remember him as he was, tall, virile, and handsome, not this lump of bloody flesh.

Our women friends entered the house, asking for Nesu's clean clothing. They prepared him for burial, washing away the blood and dressing his body in a clean tunic. We took one of his most colorful blankets from his bed and wrapped him in it.

As we completed the preparations, Father returned with priests from the Crocodile temple. They were pleased to find him ready and placed him on a pallet. With a nod, they signaled for their acolytes to carry it.

Father went to Mother. "You must come with us, Tabia."

I had never heard him speak so gently with her. "You will want to know where we bury our son."

Mother's unseeing eyes turned to Father. "He is in the belly of the crocodile."

"Not all. The priests are here to help us bury him. I will help you. So will Hagar."

The look he gave me will always haunt me. Never have I seen my father so helpless, so in need of another. I hurried to help Mother stand. The priests waited with frowns on their faces.

Before helping mother to walk behind the priests, I hurried to the corner of the room where I kept my few possessions and dug through my trunk. At the bottom, I grabbed the small bag of coins I had saved from my share of the sales of baskets and papyrus sheets.

I handed the bag to a priest. "Will this get him to the Aaru, the Field of Reeds?"

The priest measured the weight of coins within the bag in his hands. "It will help his journey through Duat and on to Aaru."

I nodded and went back to help Mother walk between my father and me.

I had given the priest everything extra I earned in the last year and a half. I no longer had any way to purchase something pretty for me or special food for Mother and Father. But Nesu, my beloved brother, would find his way to the world of beauty.

We walked a long distance through the streets of Memphis and into the wilderness. The priests had sent men ahead to dig a hole in the sand. When we arrived, the hole gaped wide.

"I cannot bury my son in that darkness," Mother howled.

"Part will reside here in the desert. The other will dwell in the belly of the crocodile." The priest's sharp tone told me my small bag of coins had not been enough. I bit back a nasty comment. *How could he lie to me like that?*

He scowled at my mother and father, tapping his long fingernails against the wooden handles that had carried the pallet. "Would you rather we had dumped him back into the Aur where all of him would live in the belly of the crocodiles?"

Mother shuddered. "No. Not that."

They lowered the pallet into the open maw, while the priest mumbled words to Sobek. I could not understand through the haze of grief that filled me. *Never would I worship that god.* Then they shoveled dirt on top of the blanket wound around Nesu.

Coldness filled me. *Would I ever feel warmth and love again. My beloved brother ... He could not breathe with the dirt over him.* I clenched my fists and watched. Numbness surrounded me.

When the hole was filled, the priest said more unintelligible words, and led us back to the city, where he left us.

It was dark before we made our way to our little home. I expected we would not eat, for I had no energy to cook and Mother could barely walk between Father and me. She could not prepare a meal. We were both overcome by sorrow. However, the fragrance of a simple soup and warm bread filled the room when we opened our door. Tali and the others had seen to our needs yet again.

Senet

After a time of grieving, Mother and I continued to collect papyrus and work with the other women weaving and making the papyrus sheets.

Mother could not return to the papyrus islands to cut the reeds for many months. Each time she tried, she would halt a distance from the riverbank and glare at the water, frozen. None of us could reach her and convince her to move forward or back.

I would finally take her hand and lead her away, speaking in soothing tones until we arrived at home. I left her there each time and rushed back to help cut the papyrus reeds.

After this happened three times, we did not tell Mother we were going to gather papyrus reeds. I would kiss her goodbye and tell her I would be back later.

I did not worry about the crocodiles, for Anta's and Nubit's sons were careful to watch for them. It helped, too, that there were many of us together. The crocodiles did not attack larger groups of people. They preferred to attack individuals and people in small groups. Ours was big enough the enormous crocodiles stayed away from us.

Although I went each time we needed more papyrus, I struggled to go to the river, knowing that crocodile waited there for us. His bellows filled my chest with a heaviness I could not ease until we were sitting around the pile of papyrus, cutting it into strips.

Mother would join us when we returned from the river, seemingly unaware that we had been to the river. How else would we have gathered so much papyrus to cut up and use?

I suspect she knew we went and stayed home preparing the water for the light green inside strips we used for the papyrus sheets.

One afternoon, after we had cut an immense pile of papyrus into slices, Mother and I returned to our home with a big urn filled with the inside strips and a gigantic pile of the dark green outer strips.

"Do not go too close to the water while you are cutting the papyrus," she said to me. "I could not bear to lose another child to the crocodiles."

"We are watchful, Mother. You know that. The boys are watchful. We have not even seen crocodiles the last few times we went."

I did not tell her we heard the big bull crocodile bellowing. I hated that crocodile. I would kill him if I could.

"Be careful," she whispered.

"You know I will."

"Did you hear Pharaoh's men are seeking women for the palace again?" Anta asked the next day as we wove papyrus sheets together in the front of her home.

"Again?" I asked. I had not seen them on the streets for many months as I fetched water from the well.

"The rumor is they need more women to serve the new queen, Senet. She is not happy with the women who are there and seeks others."

I sucked in a deep breath. I had been busy with the women making and weaving papyrus sheets for almost three years. I had not needed to watch for Pharaoh's men in the evenings when I went to the well for Mother.

"What are they looking for?" I asked.

"Young, beautiful women, like you," Samira said. "You need to be cautious."

I no longer had Nesu to help me. How could I avoid them?

"Life has become a time of watchfulness," I said, wrinkling my nose. "Watch for crocodiles. Watch for Pharaoh's men. Watch for thieves. When can I watch for something good?"

"Your time for normal things will come if you survive the next few years," Mother said. "Stay away from the crocodiles and avoid Pharaoh's men. That is most important. I would not want to lose you too."

I hugged my mother. "I will be watchful. No crocodile is going to get me."

"I worry about Pharaoh's men as well. You would be gone and I would never know why."

Each time I left home after that, I stopped to give Mother a hug and a kiss. "I love you," I said. "If I do not return, know that I will always love you."

She would hold me in a close embrace. "If Pharaoh's men take you, always remember I love you."

"Will they tell you or reimburse you for my lost labor?" I asked, hoping they would tell her, if nothing else, but none of the other mothers of the missing girls had heard from them.

"I do not know. I have never had a daughter taken by them, nor any of the daughters of the women I know. Try not to be taken."

One afternoon a few weeks later, I went to the well. Mother had cried as I left, as she had done the last times I left. I tried to look every direction as I walked toward the well, but I could not see behind me or down long alleys.

Suddenly, a voice rang out. "Stop there."

Pharaoh's men! I bit my lip and pretended he did not speak to me as I continued to walk.

"Did you not hear?" the voice growled. "I said stop." His huge paw grabbed my shoulder and turned me about.

I fought to balance my urn on my shoulder as it wobbled. Some sloshed out. I put my hands up to prevent it from falling as I stopped walking.

I pulled my urn into my arms and held it in front of me. "What do you want from me? My mother needs water."

"A brash one," the brawny man, whose dark hair had been cut short, said with a laugh.

One of Pharaoh's men. He wore the short purple kilt, identifying him as Pharaoh's man. I stepped back.

"I said, stand still," he roared, lifting his hand to slap me.

I flinched and waited for his hand to hit. It would hurt.

"Do not hit her," another of Pharaoh's men warned. "She wants her servants uninjured." This man had shaved his head bald and had as many muscles as the first.

Are muscles required to gather women for Pharaoh?

"She?" I asked. "She who?"

The men looked at each other. "Senet, if you must know," the first, short-haired man said. "Set your urn down so we can see you."

"But Mother needs her water," I protested.

"Put it down," the bald man ordered.

His voice startled me. I carefully set the urn on the side of the path. *Why had I not slumped and drooled like Nesu warned me? I have become reckless in the days since Nesu's death.*

"She may do," the first said. "Turn."

I spun in a fast circle. *Maybe they cannot see me if I move too fast.*

"Slowly," the second man barked.

I rolled my lips inward and turned slowly as ordered. *Why did I not drool?*

"She will do. Senet will like her mouthiness."

"And Pharaoh will like her looks."

I clutched my hands. I did not want to have Pharaoh look at me. What would my mother and father do?

"My parents lost my brother to a crocodile last year. I am all they have left," I cried. "Can you not find another?"

The men glanced at each other.

"I am sorry for your parents," the short-haired man said. "But we have no choice. We must take you to Senet. We have found no other women today and she demands more."

"Can you send a message to my parents? My mother will be sick with worry."

Bald head shook his head. "Perhaps Senet will give you permission to send a message."

What good would it do to send her a message? Mother could not read. I could not write.

I clenched my jaw and refused to cry as they led me toward the palace, pulling me by the arm, remembering Senet did not want me bruised. My urn still perched on the street. Someone would find it. I would cry later, when no one could see me. Perhaps I could convince Senet to send me home to my parents.

Bald and Short Hair led me into the palace through a back gate I did not know existed. But I spent little time near the palace.

I kept my head down, hardly looking at my surroundings. All I could think of was what Mother would think when she came looking for me and found our urn abandoned on the side of the path.

I bit the inside of my lip. *I tried to be aware, Mother. I tried to watch in every direction. They came upon me suddenly. I did not see them until it was too late.*

I lifted my head. Perhaps I could find an escape.

The men led me through a maze of halls until at last an older woman met them with her hands on her hips. "Men do not belong in these rooms."

Short Hair ducked his head. "Senet required a new servant. We have found a woman for her."

The woman stalked around me, pulling at my skirt, touching me in places no one had touched me since my mother touched me as a baby.

Leave me alone. You have no right to touch me there. She unbound my dirty, dark hair, tutting with each movement.

I tried to flinch away from her, but she pinched my butt cheek and hissed, "Be still."

So I endured the indignity of her probing fingers.

"You did not touch her?" Her lips flattened.

Baldy and Short Hair gasped. "No, madam!"

Her curt nod sent them on their way, almost running from her presence. I wanted to join them, but her gaze froze me to the floor.

"What are you called?" the woman asked.

"H-H-Hagar," I stammered.

"Well, H-H-Hager, come with me." She turned to stride down a hall.

I lifted my chin. *If I am to be here, I will not shrink.* "It is Hagar."

The woman stopped and glared at me. "Then why did you not say so at first?"

"I was afraid." I frowned at her.

"And you are not afraid now?" The woman stepped close and took my chin, lifting it.

"No." I stiffened my back. "You can do nothing more to hurt my mother and father. They lost my brother to the grandfather crocodile last year. Now they lose me to the palace. What more can you do to them?"

"You do not fear for yourself?" Her eyes widened and she stepped back half a step.

"I am dead to my parents. What more can you do?"

The woman tipped her head back and cackled. "You will do," she said through her laughter. "Senet will like you. I am Ketet. I am responsible for you and all the others those ruffians bring to Pharaoh's household."

I nodded my head. "Ketet. You must be busy."

Her head tipped back to roar with laughter once more. "You have no idea." She pulled a cloth from a small bag hanging over her shoulder and wiped her eyes. "You will do. Come with me."

Ketet spun on her heel and strode away, never swiveling her head to see if I followed. *Sure of herself.* I trotted behind, only now seeing the golden figures standing in the hallway.

I inhaled sharply as we passed a huge golden crocodile standing on its hind feet, its tail extending back to balance it, and its mouth wide open. Sharp teeth glistened in the light.

"What?" Ketet asked.

"The crocodile looks so real."

"It should," she said, turning to stride down the hall. "It is real. Pharaoh had it dipped in gold to keep it forever with us as a reminder of what happens to us if we disobey."

"He would not," I gasped.

"He would," Ketet said and continued her march through the halls.

I shuddered as I followed her. I had hoped that fear would not cause me trouble within the walls of the palace. However, there it set, a crocodile almost as big as the one that ate my brother and stayed close when we cut papyrus. I could not free myself of the crocodiles.

Ketet led me to a bathing pool. "Take off those dirty clothes. Senet will not want you in your filth and stench."

I sniffed myself. I did not stink. I smelled of papyrus and Mother's cooking. I did not argue, though. Steam rose from the water. I had heard of these hot baths but had only experienced an occasional wash with a cloth with warmed water to wash away the dirt. I removed my dress and other clothing, too proud to try to cover myself. She would not see my distress at showing my young body to others. At Ketet's nod, I stepped into the deep pool.

The warmth surrounded me. It felt like I had gone to the Field of Reeds, causing me to search for Nesu. Surely he was here too. Then I recognized what I did. The pool was empty. I shuddered. Nesu would never be here with me again.

I ducked beneath the water, enjoying the warmth of the water. When I pushed up again, Ketet waited with a small urn filled with soap.

"Wash your hair with this," she ordered.

I took the urn and dipped soap out, using it to wash my hair. I welcomed the unknown opulence. After I submerged my head to rinse my hair, Ketet held out the urn again.

"Once more," she said.

I did as she suggested, washing and rinsing my hair a second time.

She then handed me another urn filled with soap and a cloth. "Now your body."

I did as she asked again. Once I was clean, she held a large towel up so I could dry myself. I had not smelled this good in all my fourteen years.

A young servant entered with a stack of clothing. Ketet picked through the clothing and chose a short, sheer shift made of linen and handed it to me.

I slipped it over my head. The shift was soft, softer than any dress I had ever worn before. I sighed. I did not expect to be treated well. I did not know what to expect. The servant combed and brushed my long, dark hair, twisted it onto my head, and pinned it up.

Pinned up hair made sense to me. It would not get in food or fall into my eyes when pinned up. I had often pinned it up when I worked with the women cutting papyrus and forming the sheets.

Ketet handed me soft slippers, then led me down another hall. Our slippers shushed across the stone floor. At a door, Ketet knocked.

A servant opened the door and peeped out, her dark eyes all that could be seen.

"I have another one for Senet," Ketet murmured.

The servant huffed, and at a sound from a woman inside, pulled the door open.

Ketet entered and gestured for me to follow.

I peered at the floor, not wanting to seem rude. I had heard that the queen did not want low class people like me looking at her.

But Ketet touched my back. "Look up, Senet wants to see your beautiful face."

"Who are you and where did you come from?" the regal woman in front of me asked.

"I am Hagar. I live along the Aur in a poor section of the city. Who are you?" I responded.

Her eyebrows twisted, and her head jerked back. "Do you not know your queen? I am Senet, wife of Pharaoh."

I ducked my head. "I did not know we were coming to you. I thought Ketet would take me to some other lady in the women's quarters."

"I may yet send you to another," Senet said sternly.

She glided in a circle looking me. Her long skirt swished against the floor she moved. I turned my head to follow her movement, but Ketet growled my name and I remained still.

"What do you seek?" I asked.

"A girl who can obey," Senet said, still circling me.

"And if I cannot, will you return me home to my parents?"

"Why would you want to leave all this to return to the hovel you call home?"

I swallowed the sudden lump in my throat. It had been more than a year, and thoughts of Nesu still brought me to tears. "My brother is gone. My parents will be alone if I do not return."

"Oh? Did Pharaoh take him into his army?"

"I would have him in Pharaoh's army if I could change things." I lifted my head and stared at Senet. "He leapt off a barge to rescue the owner's little girl. Before he could get back on, Grandfather Crocodile got him."

The servant in the room gasped. Senet tilted her head to the side and looked at me through narrowed eyes. "Is this true?"

"It is," I replied. I rubbed at the tears on my cheeks. "The crocodile took him from the waist down. We buried the rest. Now Mother and Father will be alone without either of us to help provide for them."

Senet returned to her seat and frowned at me for a long time. At last she spoke. "That is tragic. I will send a guard to your parents and tell them what happened to you. He will take them a bag of coins to help care for them."

I fell to her feet. "You would do that for me? Why not allow me to return?"

"You please me." She ran her fingers along my cheek. "I am in need of another servant. You will do." Senet turned to Ketet. "Bring her a longer shift to mark her status as my servant."

Ketet bowed and backed out of the room.

"You will serve me here in my rooms." Senet waved toward the other servant. "Uat will show you where to sleep and what to do." She waved her hands. "Go. Return to me in an hour."

Uat led me deeper into Senet's rooms. She led me past a vast bed covered with colorful linen blankets.

"That is Senet's bed. You are never to touch it."

I gawked at the furnishings in the room. Burnished copper mirrors, shining tables and chairs made of ebony, and glittering jewels sitting on her dressing table were all more elegant and beautiful than I had ever seen. "Not even to straighten the blankets?"

"No. A slave comes to straighten the bed. You are not to touch it."

I nodded. "There is nothing here for me. It is too elegant. Where do we sleep?"

"We? I sleep there." Uat pointed to a closet. A thin pallet lay on its floor. "You will sleep with the other servants. But now, we have things to do. Pharaoh will soon come to see Senet. We must set out her gown and prepare to dress her."

I nodded and gazed about the room, confused. I did not see any dresses hanging along the wall, no chests against the walls.

"Where are her clothes?" I asked.

Uat peered at me. "What do you mean?"

She thinks me a dolt or a stupid, poor woman. I am poor.

"Where does Senet keep her clothing? I see no hooks, no trunks," I said, looking at the room.

"Senet is a wealthy woman, the wife of Pharaoh. Her clothing is not here. She has a room just for her clothing." Disdain dripped from Uat's tongue.

Enough. "I am a poor girl and have lived with my family in a small hovel. I did not ask to come here. Your men took me off the street. What do I know of life in the palace?" I lifted my chin and gazed at Uat down my nose. "I am able to learn. Senet could have sent me home to my mother. She did not. Instead, she gave you the responsibility to teach me." I set my hands on my hips. "So teach me."

Uat stuttered and blustered, then pivoted on her slippered heel and led me through a curtain.

I refused to let Uat see my amazement, but I leaned toward the beautiful silk dresses hanging on hooks.

"Do not touch. You do not want to get Senet's dresses dirty," Uat growled.

"My hands are clean. Ketet insisted I bathe after your men brought me here."

"Why do you keep saying it was my men who brought you to court? I had nothing to do with it."

"I did not ask them to bring me here. They are part of Pharaoh's household. So are you. That means you have a part in it."

"I have no more part in those men bringing you here than you did. Senet is always searching for servants. Servants do not stay here long." Uat's voice softened, briefly.

"How long have you been with her?" I offered her a small smile.

Uat blew the air from her lungs. "A month. I fear you will take my place and she will send me to a priest or to work for one of the other women."

I shuddered. "I would not desire to be given to a priest. I am a woman."

"And priests use women differently, for more than servants." Her eyebrows lifted, suggesting more.

My stomach reeled. "I definitely do not want the priests to take me. Better to go to another woman, or better yet, to go home to my parents." *I want nothing to do with priests, especially Sobek's priests.*

Uat peered at me, touching the center of her chest with her palm. "You do not understand yet, do you?"

I gawked at her numbly.

"You will never go home to your parents. You belong to the court. Senet will not allow you to spread gossip about her or Pharaoh."

"I would never gossip!"

"No? You would not tell your friends where you have been? Tell them about this room?" Uat lifted her eyebrows.

I chewed on the inside of my lip. "I may tell them of this room."

"Senet will never give you the opportunity."

"Where will I go when Senet no longer wants me?" My legs suddenly weakened.

"I do not know. I only know women and girls disappear from court, never to be seen again."

I absorbed a gulp and lifted my chin. "Then I must never cause Senet to dislike me."

Fight

Senet swept into her rooms before we had everything laid out. Uat cringed away from Senet's hand. Did she expect a slap? A hit?

It did not come.

"I had to show Hagar where you keep your clothing and jewelry. It takes time to teach a new servant," Uat stammered as she smoothed her shift.

"Did Ketet bring a shift appropriate for my servant yet?" Senet asked, eying the shift I still wore.

I shook my head. "No, mistress. I have not seen Ketet since she left your presence."

Senet frowned, besmirching her beautiful face. "She should be here already."

A rap on the door announced Ketet's presence. "Three women required my time. I apologize, mistress Senet, for taking so long to return to your rooms with the appropriate shift. Nabukha required something of me."

"Nabukha." Senet spat the name as though Ketet had given her poison.

Ketet lifted her shoulder.

"Give Hagar the shift so she can help dress me. Pharaoh should come to the common room soon. I need to be ready."

Ketet handed me the shift. I looked for a place to change.

"Just change already," Senet growled.

"Here?" I squeaked.

When both Ketet and Uat nodded, I pulled my shift off over my head. I hurried to pull the new shift on, not wanting them to see how uncomfortable nakedness in front of others made me.

"That was not so bad," Senet said. "Uat, is that what you expect me to wear?" She pointed at the dress and other clothing items lying on the bed.

"You do not want to wear this dress?" Uat asked, snatching the dress from the bed.

"The dress is fine," Senet said. "I do not want that headdress, and those jewels do not match."

Uat turned to me. "See. I told you they did not go together."

I rolled my lips inward. She had said nothing about it to me. Actually, I had questioned her choice of headdress and jewels.

"I will get another for you," I said, grabbing the headdress.

As I passed Senet, I saw her eyes narrow. Did she know Uat had passed the blame to me?

In the room that held Senet's clothing, I found the headdress I originally suggested, the one with the same color in it as the dress. I took it back into Senet's room, where Uat had helped her out of her clothing. Ketet had left them alone.

"That is better," Senet said in a voice that carried no emotion. "Help Uat put oils and ointments on me."

I set the headdress on the dressing table. Uat poured some oil into my open hand and I massaged it into Senet's legs and arms while Uat rubbed it into Senet's body.

Uat dipped ointment from another urn and dropped it in my palm. "Massage this behind her knees, ears, and at her elbows," she ordered.

I dipped a bit onto my finger and sniffed. It smelled of jasmine. I rubbed a small dot behind Senet's knees.

"Is that enough?" Senet asked, staring down at me from her stool.

"In my experience, a little bit goes a long way," I said.

"In your vast experience," Uat snarled.

"I may have lived in a poor hovel, but my mother taught me how to be beautiful and how to entice the young men."

"And did you leave a 'young man' behind pining for you?" Uat asked. Her nose wrinkled.

"No. There is one who may miss me, but I am too young to entice men."

Bau. He may miss me. He spoke kind words to me the last time he helped me carry water from the well.

"Too young?" Senet glanced at me sharply. "How old are you?"

"I am but fourteen years my last naming day."

"Fourteen," Senet mused. "My mother brought me here to entice Pharaoh when I was but twelve years." She sniffed softly. "I will try the smaller amount today. If Pharaoh complains, you will be beaten, Hagar."

I closed my eyes, trying to quell the quivering in my stomach. I had no way of knowing such things occurred at court. I thought they only beat criminals.

I slowly let my breath escape as I dipped another small daub of the ointment and rubbed it behind Senet's other knee. Then I moved to anoint behind her ears, then her wrists. I took her hand.

"May I anoint your wrists with a tiny amount?"

"Uat has never anointed my wrists."

"Mother taught me to touch beautiful smelling ointments at our pulse points. It brings out the fragrance as our bodies warm in the presence of a man."

Senet lifted her eyebrows and turned her eyes on Uat as she held out her wrists for me to anoint.

I rolled my lips inward. I did not want to cause trouble for Uat. She had been with Senet for a time. She did not want to lose her privileges. I could not blame her.

Still, when I peeked toward Uat, her eyes were black with anger. I did not want an enemy, especially on my first day in the women's quarters. I wanted to shake my head and apologize, but Senet was making more demands.

"You must hurry. Help me with my small clothes, quickly."

I frowned at the arrangement of clothing on the bed and found what could only be small clothes and held them so Senet could step into them.

We continued dressing her, putting on layers of gauzy shawls over her bright blue dress.

Uat brushed Senet's hair until it shone, then pinned it in curls around her head with jeweled pins she found in a box on the table.

Using brushes and her fingers, Uat painted Senet's eyes with black ocher. When I stepped back to see, rather than the fearful face I expected, she looked strikingly beautiful.

I lifted the headdress from its place on the table and held it over her head. "Now?" I asked.

Senet nodded, and I moved to set it on her head.

"Not like that," Uat growled and took it from me. "I do not know what Senet is thinking, asking a peasant with no understanding of royalty to dress her." She spoke under her breath, as though Senet could not hear.

"You also came from the country, a peasant with no knowledge," Senet said. "Show Hagar how it is done. You may not always be here."

Uat refrained from speaking whatever retort she had on her tongue and straightened the headdress and showed me how to place it on Senet's head. "Like this."

I watched closely. "I have not seen those before. Thank you for showing me."

Uat's jaw tightened, but she did not respond.

When the headdress settled firmly on Senet's head, she poked her feet toward me.

I glanced at Uat.

"She needs slippers," Uat said, reaching for jeweled earrings.

Before I put the slippers on Senet's feet, however, I dipped my fingers into the pot of oil and rubbed it into Senet's feet. She closed her eyes and groaned in delight.

"Why have you never put oils on my feet?" Senet asked Uat.

Uat's eyes bulged and I could hear her grinding her teeth as she hung a jeweled necklace about Senet's neck. "Because your feet are as dry as the desert and stink," she mumbled so low I almost missed it. Uat then tied strings of jewels on Senet's wrists.

"Oils will help soften your feet," I said as I set her slipper on her foot, then dipped into the pot of oil and rubbed it into her other foot.

After I put the second slipper on Senet's feet, she closed her eyes and smiled.

"Uat, be certain Hagar is still here when I return. I will want her to help me prepare for bed." Senet stood and picked up a bag that matched her dress.

Uat had dumped it out before Senet arrived and replaced the square of linen and a small pot of grease for her lips.

Senet slipped the bag over her shoulder and breezed out the door.

I stared at the closing door. How did I get here, dressing Pharaoh's favorite wife? I shook my head and surveyed the room. "Is it always like this?"

Uat turned to me and barked at me. "Just what was all that about? Putting oil on her feet! How could you stand touching her dry, stinky feet? And the doe-eyed, 'I have never done that before?' How could you undermine me like that?"

"I came from my parents' hovel today. I left a water urn on the side of the path for my mother to find and learn I am never coming home."

"Oh, your poor parents." Uat's voice dripped sarcasm. "You have come to the palace to live a life of luxury. You have caught the eye of the most influential woman in the land, and you whine about living here."

My voice dropped. "I did not want to live here. I was happy living with my parents. And what was that comment you made about me choosing the wrong headdress? You chose it. Not me. I tried to tell you it was wrong."

"What do you know about anything?" Uat spat.

"I know what headdress looks good with that dress," I fumed.

"You know nothing. You are a low girl from a hovel by the river. A fisherman's daughter." Her scowl could have dried the sea. She slapped me on the arm and turned away from me.

"Why did you do that?" I cried and hit her in the back.

She turned and grabbed my hair and yanked it. "You are a little brat."

I grabbed her hair and pulled it. "You are a cheat and a liar."

She took my hair and jerked, ripping hair from my head.

Before, I only resented her actions. Now anger consumed me. I tugged on her hair, dragging a fist full from her head. She turned and fought back. I grabbed her arm and held it away from me. She hit me with the other hand. I slapped her.

She grabbed my hand. I turned and freed my arm from her hand, then twisted her arm behind her back, as Nesu had taught me. She let out a yelp.

"You little cur," she cried.

"Better a cur than a liar."

She kicked back and caught my knee. I held on to her hand, but she twisted away and scratched me.

"Harlot!" Uat screamed.

"Better than a whore," I growled. I wadded her dress front in my hand and pulled.

The fabric in her dress gave way, tearing down the front of it. "My dress," she howled and reached for mine.

I twisted away and punched her in the stomach. She doubled over.

I bent over and put my hands on my knees, panting. Surely it was enough, but she reached up and clawed at me, gripping the front of my dress.

I lurched back, and a ripping sound filled the room. "This is my new dress," I cried. My dress had ripped as far as the width of my hand. "Why did you do that?" I yelped.

"Why do I do anything?" she said, scratching my arm with her long fingernails. "Because I hate you."

Long red streaks appeared on my arm. "I did nothing to you." I kicked her in the shins.

"Nothing but make me look bad in front of Senet." She reached for my hair, but I spun away.

Uat grabbed me and punched me in the face.

I will get her!

Just then, the door opened and three men marched through.

"What is this noise?" the biggest shouted. He waved his hands and the other two men grabbed us, pinning our arms to our sides.

Uat hissed at me. I clenched my fist and growled.

"Is this the way lady servants of the Lady Senet behave?" the first man asked.

"She started it, Yafeu," Uat cried, forcing crocodile tears to run down her cheeks.

"Ha! You rushed at me, pulled my hair and scratched me. Look at my arms," I blazed, showing my arms. "You have no scratches on you."

"You are both a terrible mess," Yafeu said, his voice low and dangerous. "What will Senet think when she returns with Pharaoh?"

My eyes opened wide. "She will return with Pharaoh?"

"What do you think? She will return with other women?" Uat's sarcasm scraped against my wounds.

"How would I know? I know nothing of the goings on of the woman's court." My voice dropped to a mutter.

"You listen to me. I was told to teach you," Uat grumbled.

"But you did not teach me. You did things wrong on purpose and blamed me." My voice lifted.

"And you tried to outshine me. Who puts oil on their feet?" Uat shouted.

The man holding her arms let one go and put a hand over her mouth.

"That is enough!" Yafeu yelled.

"But I..." I stuttered.

"Both of you. I have had enough of this. Look at you. Your hair is a mess. Your dresses are torn and your bodies are showing."

I peered down at my dress and gasped.

"You are covered in scratches," Yafeu continued, pointing at me. "I do not know your name, but you are my responsibility. Settle down. Both of you!" He waved at the men. "Let them go."

They released my arms and I lowered my eyes. "My name is Hagar. Your men brought me here this morning. Ketet brought me to Senet."

Yafeu nodded. "Ketet told me of you. She said you would be a welcome addition to the women's court." He raised his eyebrows. "But not like this."

Yafeu shook his head with closed eyes. "Why am I stuck here in the women's court with women who fight like cats? Put on clean dresses and clean up this mess."

The room was a mess. I pulled the edges of my dress together. "I have no other dress. Ketet brought me only one."

"Uat, give her one of your dresses until Ketet can replace it," Yafeu ordered. He lifted a finger. "One of your new dresses."

Uat bent her head. "Yes, Yafeu."

"I will return to check on you before Senet returns with Pharaoh. This room will be neat and tidy by then. And you will both be here, dressed in appropriate dresses." He pointed a finger at Uat and waited for her to bow her head and mumble agreement before he pointed his long finger at me.

"Yes, sir," I said, wincing."

"No. More. Fighting. You are here to serve Senet. If you cannot do that, I am sure there are pots to scrub in the kitchen, or clothing to wash. Do not disobey me."

I ducked my head and nodded. "Yes, sir."

"I am not sir. I am Yafeu," he growled.

"Yes, Yafeu," I said.

"Yes, Yafeu," Uat said.

As Yafeu turned to walk out, Uat stuck her tongue out at me. I rolled my lips inward and sucked in a deep breath. I would not allow her to force me out. I did not like scrubbing pots or washing clothing.

Uat bent to pick up Senet's discarded clothing from the floor. "Some days it is a nightmare here. I will offer her three dresses before she chooses one, then I have to find a headdress, shawls, and jewelry to match."

"Such an interesting problem to have," I muttered as I closed the pots of oil and jasmine ointment.

That night after Pharaoh had left Senet's apartments, she called Uat and me in. She frowned at us over her folded arms.

"I heard there was a problem here after I left."

I bowed my head and pressed my lips together. I did not wish to be the one to tell her what had happened.

"Not a problem, really," Uat said, flicking a glance at me. "We were overly enthusiastic in our cleaning after you left. We were making some noise and Yafeu came in to see what was going on."

I gulped. *I could not lie so glibly.*

Senet stared at me. "Is that what happened?"

I swallowed. "It is."

"And how did you get those scratches on your arms, Hagar?"

I rolled my lips in.

"The jewels caught on her arms as she returned them to their boxes," Uat said quickly.

Senet's eyes opened wide. "I thought I wore all the jewels you had sitting out."

"No," Uat lied. "There were some here you did not wear, hidden beneath a dress. They scratched Hagar's arms."

Senet turned her glare on me. "Is that what happened?"

My stomach tightened. "Yes." Even I could not hear my words.

"What did you say?" Senet asked, her voice rising. "Speak up. Is that what happened?"

I inhaled deeply and forced my voice to work. "Yes. That is what happened. I did not know jewels would scratch me like that."

"Is that a different dress you wear, Hagar? I thought you wore a simple shift."

"No," Uat said, lying once again. "That is the dress Ketet brought to her before you left."

I swallowed the comment on my tongue. I still wore the shift Uat had given me after Yafeu had ordered it. Ketet had brought me another moments before Senet arrived and I did not have time to change.

"Uat, I have told you before that lying is not acceptable in the women's court. Do you not think Yafeu would not share with me exactly what happened and why he came into my rooms? I heard about your torn shifts, your hair in disarray, the scratches on your arms, Hagar, and the screeching and screaming that emitted from my apartment." Senet lifted a finger and pointed it toward Uat. "You have no more chances. Ketet will come for you tonight."

Uat fell to the floor at Senet's feet. "I apologize, Senet. I feared you would be harsh and send me away if I admitted to my mistakes. Hagar argued that the headdress I chose would not match the dress I had out for you." Her muffled voice rose from the place on the floor where she lay.

"How could a woman, a girl really, from the country know more than me? I have been here for so long. When she reminded me of it, my stomach filled with anger and I slapped her."

"You were new once," Senet said.

"I was. But I came from a household with money, not from a hovel near the river."

"And?" Senet's question dripped with regret.

Uat lifted her head from the floor. "I am better than her. How can she know any of those things? And what gives her the right to hit me when I hit her?"

I shrunk into myself, hoping Senet would not notice me.

"She had the audacity to hit you back?" Sarcasm filled Senet's voice.

Uat obviously did not hear it, for she vigorously nodded her head. "And when I pulled strands of her hair from her head, she yanked mine back. Then she kicked me and I scratched ... her ..." Uat's voice dropped away as she noticed Senet's cold eyes staring at her and a vein pulsing on her neck.

"Do you not think it was awful of her to fight back?" Uat whimpered.

"No, I do not," Senet said in a carefully controlled tone. "I tasked you to teach her what to do, not to reprimand her, nor to become angry when she suggested something you do not like."

"I just did not —"

Senet chopped her hand down in front of her to cut Uat off. "You do not like to touch my feet. I heard your comment. It embarrassed you that Hagar put oil on them." Her voice hardened. "I would have overlooked that, but not a fight here in my rooms needing Yafeu and his men to break it up. You have been here longer. You know how things go."

She turned to me. "Even coming from a small home along the river, you should know it is wrong to fight in the women's court."

"I did not, but it felt wrong," I admitted.

Senet inhaled deeply and let the air out noisily. "I do not know what got into you two. I had high hopes for you both."

I bit my lip. "Mistress," I whispered. *What high hopes? Could I still meet her needs?*

"Speak up. No need to whisper here," Senet huffed.

"I am still new here. Uat has taught me much today." Like how to fight with another girl. "But not enough for me to care for your needs alone. Can you give her another chance?"

Uat gasped.

Senet stared from me to Uat. "I do not know if I can trust the two of you together."

Uat flinched away. "I can work with Hagar," she stammered. "I will teach her what to do to take care of your needs."

"And you will hold nothing back, thinking it will be insurance to keep you here longer?" Senet peered into Uat's face, holding her eyes until Uat dropped hers.

"Yes, Mistress Senet. I will teach her everything. I will not hold back."

"And neither of you will fight again?" Senet's eyes turned to me, then back to Uat.

"N-n-no, Mistress Senet," I said.

"No Mistress," Uat agreed. "We will not fight again."

Senet groaned loudly. "No more chances. Especially you, Uat. You have received more than your share of chances. No. More."

I clasped my hands in front of me. "Thank you."

Uat lay her hand over her heart. "I will not let you down."

"I have heard that before," Senet said in a stern voice. "Do not make me repent of this."

"No, Mistress," Uat said, bowing to the floor and bumping her head on the stones.

I knelt to imitate her.

HAGAR, MOTHER OF SORROWS

"You do not need to bow as low as Uat," Senet said. "Now help me remove this headdress. It is heavy."

Betrayal

U at was careful to teach me all that Senet needed in a servant. We helped her bathe in the mornings, brushed her hair out and curled it. Once I braided Senet's hair, then curled it to her head.

"What is this you have done to my hair?" Senet asked.

"I braided it," I said. "My mother would braid hers to keep it out of the way when she worked over the stove. Hair burns, and Mother did not want her hair to catch fire."

"Wise woman. But this is not a simple braid?"

"No, Mistress Senet. I made small braids and curled them."

"It looks nice on you," Uat said. "Look." She held up a polished circle of copper.

Senet turned her head to the side and held the mirror in front of her, then off to the side. "You are correct," she said. "This does look good. You may complete the rest of my hair."

I nodded and plucked up another small hank of hair and brushed and braided it.

"Uat, you should help," Senet said.

Uat picked up a brush and braided the other side of Senet's hair.

When we finished, Senet lifted the polished brass mirror and peered at her reflection. With a nod, she handed the mirror to me. "This will do for today. I shall see what the other women say. More importantly, I shall see how Pharaoh reacts to this style."

I gulped. I had forgotten that everything we did was to gain favor in Pharaoh's eyes.

"He will love this," Uat said with a grin and sparkling eyes.

We walked back to Senet's apartment with her, laughing at her little jokes. Uat and I had become fast friends after our fight, working together to make Senet look good. We brought her food from the kitchens in the morning and were there at night to help her undress.

Pharaoh loved her hair in those braids, and soon other servants came to us to ask how to dress their ladies in curled braids. Uat and I showed them using each other as examples. Soon all the women in the women's court wore their hair in small braids that were curled and held with jeweled pins.

One night, when we stepped from our rooms into Senet's, she and Pharaoh were on her bed, rolling around. My face reddened and I backed away silently.

Uat took longer to return to our room. "Why did you leave?"

"What took you so long to leave?" I retorted. "That is private."

"How would you know?"

"Mother and Father did that in our small home. They taught us to look away, even though we were in the same room. It is private between a husband and wife."

Uat snorted. "Between a man and a woman. We watch sometimes."

I gaped at her. "Why?"

She shrugged. "How else will we learn how to be with a man?"

I swallowed, then swallowed again. "Mother taught me I will learn that on my marriage night. What happens between a man and a woman is private."

"You never watched them?" Uat asked. "I would have."

"Not my mother and father! Mother would have beat you if she saw you watching." I remembered the one night Nesu had peeked. Mother had beaten him with a wooden spoon. I would never watch after that.

"I would not know," Uat said with a sniff. "My parents never slept in the same room as me." She coughed. "They did not live in the same house as me. I have lived as a servant for as long as I could remember."

"You do not remember living with your parents?"

"They were servants to the same family as me. Mother and I served the mistress. Father served the master. He drove the horses that pulled the carriage." Uat thrust out her chest and lifted her chin. "Father was important in that household."

"Why did you leave then?"

Uat's eyes dropped to the floor and her posture crumpled. "Father was ordered to race the carriage, turning the corners too fast, to get the master to an important meeting in time."

She bit the inside of her lip. "The horses could not turn the carriage around one corner safely. The carriage tipped over and caught Father between the carriage and the street as the horses dragged it. His body was a mangled mess before the horses stopped."

"Oh, Uat," I cried and held out my arms to console her in an embrace.

She shook her head and lifted her chin. "The master was injured, too, but not badly, only a broken arm. However, his anger was so great he returned home in a rage. He wanted to send Mother and I to the streets immediately."

Uat took a deep breath.

"Did he?" I whispered.

"Not then. The mistress convinced him they could sell our services to others, rather than lose our service and the coins they would make."

A tear slipped from my eyes. *My parents were still together, even without Nesu and me.*

Uat flipped her hair back away from her face. "I do not know where they sold Mother. One day she was gone. A few days after that, they ordered me to gather anything I claimed as mine. The steward led me from their house here. They sold me to the women's court."

"Did you serve someone else before Senet?"

"I served another lady first. I was young, like you."

I lifted my eyebrows. "You are not much older than me."

"Five years. I am nineteen." Her hands settled on her hips. "It did not take long for Senet to see me, though. She took me from the other lady and brought me to serve her when Pharaoh married her." Uat shook her head. "Before then, she was like all the other women, except Nabukha."

"Nabukha?"

I remembered her sitting in the gathering room apart from the silly chattering of the women. We servants perched on the edges of the room, waiting for a signal from our mistress to do her bidding.

"Is she the older woman who sits away from the younger women? She sits so straight. Everyone respects that woman."

"Yes," Uat sneered. "They must respect her. She was Pharaoh's first wife until she gave him only girl babies. About three years ago, he left Nabukha for a younger, more beautiful woman, Senet."

"How sad for Nabukha," I murmured. I could not imagine Father setting Mother aside because she did not give him more children or even if she gave him only girls. They would mourn the loss of their children together.

"Ha. Nabukha is well treated. She does not mind giving way to a younger, more beautiful woman."

"I would care if it were me set aside," I whispered.

"They will never set you aside. You will never marry. Servants in the women's court do not marry."

I gasped. "Never?"

"Who would we marry? We never leave the walls of the court. When would we see a man who would want us?"

"Then why do you watch Pharaoh and Senet?" I asked. "If you will never be with a man, why watch to learn?"

"I can hope it will happen," Uat mumbled.

"And if you get a child with in you? What then?"

"I will have it removed. We cannot have children. Yafeu would send us from the court."

I swallowed. "Not have children? Never?" *Could I bear never having children?*

"That is what I was told. Never."

Only Pharaoh's women and those of his leading people can have children. Not those of us who serve them. It is unfair. I did not choose to be here. I want to go home. I want to live with my parents. To see Bau again. I want to have children. Not yet, of course, I am only fourteen, but sometime I do. Sometime soon.

Thoughts like these ran through my head for months as I helped dress and serve Senet each day. I did not like to be denied my right as a woman.

However, Uat had told me untruths before. She did it 'because it is amusing,' she said when I caught her telling lies. Amusing to see how I would react? Amusing to cause me to fear and worry. Perhaps we could leave the court sometime. Perhaps we could marry and have children.

I could not trust the things Uat told me.

Senet gave us time to do as we wished in our room while Pharaoh and she were together, but we needed to be available if they wanted more wine or food. We played games together or Uat taught me to read. Words on a scroll of papyrus were like magic. I often wondered about the scrolls. Were these scrolls made by my mother and our friends? Had I made this one?

I liked to think Mother had helped make the papyrus. It brought me closer to her. Sometimes, after everyone else slept, I would take out the scroll of papyrus and hold it close to my chest, trying to feel my mother's love from it.

Those days brought a loneliness I did not expect. I thought I had become accustomed to living away from home. Living in the women's court was different from living at home had ever been. I did not cook or clean the dishes. I was not required to clean my clothing or the floors. Slaves did those chores for us.

I helped Senet with whatever she needed. I ate well and slept in a warm bed. Only Uat shared our little room. We never worried about rain leaking through the roof. And I never feared Grandfather Crocodile. He lived in the Aur while I lived safely in the women's court of the palace.

Then, things changed. One night when Pharaoh came to spend time with Senet, Uat asked me to cover for her.

"I want to visit a friend. Senet will not need both of us. She and Pharaoh will be busy," she said. "Tell Senet I am ill with a headache."

"What will you do for me?" I asked.

"Oh Hagar. Should you not do this for a friend?"

"Perhaps I should, but you are asking me to say you are sleeping. What will you do for me?"

After thinking a bit, Uat agreed. "I will bring you a special treat from the kitchen."

I liked the sweets the cook made and readily agreed.

Senet did not call for wine or food that evening. After Pharaoh left, she called and I hurried in to see to her needs.

"Where is Uat?" Senet asked, looking past me.

"She has a headache tonight. She asked me to see to your needs alone tonight."

"A headache? I have something that will help it." She searched for the remedy.

"She sleeps. She said sleep would solve her headache better than anything." My heart pounded at the lie.

Senet sank back into her seat in front of her dressing table. "If you think sleep is enough ..."

"Uat said it would be." I unpinned the curls and undid her braids so I could brush out her hair. "She says she has had headaches like this before and sleep helped heal her best."

Senet glared into the mirror. "I suppose you can get me ready for bed alone."

I grinned. "I think I can do that. Uat and I often get in each other's way."

I poured a cup of wine for Senet to drink while I brushed her hair and loosely braided it for sleeping. After helping her into a sleeping robe, I washed her face and rubbed oils on her body and feet, helping her prepare to sleep while she lay on her bed.

"Your hands are soothing," Senet said. She closed her eyes and slept.

I tip-toed from the room and found my pallet. I could do these things on my own, but it bothered me to tell untruths. I picked up the scroll I had been reading and held it close.

Mother, did you help create this? Did you earn some coins for it? I miss you and Father.

Sadness overwhelmed me. I had not missed my parents like this in a long time. I was grateful Uat had left. I did not want to explain to her my sagging body and unwillingness to talk. She would understand. She sometimes grew quiet, thinking of and missing her mother.

I lay down, thinking of home. I wondered what Mother and Father were doing. I hoped they rolled in their bed, working to create another child.

Uat slipped into our room sometime later and quietly undressed. I sleepily opened my eyes as she set a cake beside my bed. She sat at our dressing table to clean her face.

"Thank you, Hagar," she whispered. "Did Senet question you?"

"I told her you had a headache and were sleeping it off. She did not question me more." I watched her through half-open eyes, more asleep than awake. The cake could wait.

"Good. You earned your cake."

"Did you enjoy your time out?" I asked.

I could hear the smile in her voice. "I did."

"Good. I am tired. Tell me more tomorrow." I turned over and slid back into sleep.

We resumed our routines the next day, caring for Senet's needs.

"Is your headache better this morning?" Senet asked Uat the next morning.

"It is. Sleep helps me."

"I did not know you suffered from headaches," Senet said, touching Uat's forehead.

"I have had some lately, after we go to bed," Uat said, rubbing her head.

I did more for Senet that day, as she wanted Uat to get over her headache.

When Pharaoh came back to spend time with Senet the next time, Uat asked me to cover for her again.

Senet became suspicious of Uat's inconvenient headaches. After she did not come in with me to help the fourth time, Senet insisted on taking her a powder to help.

I tried to deflect her. "Uat is sleeping off her headache. If you wake her, she will not be well enough to serve you in the morning."

Senet sighed and handed me the healing powder. "If she wakes during the night, give her this. I do not like having my servants sick."

I took the powder and slipped it into the bag at my waist. "I am certain she will take it tonight. I will give it to her."

My words satisfied Senet for that night, but when it happened twice more, Senet could no longer be distracted.

"I must see to my servant. She never had headaches like this before. What is causing her illness?"

What could I tell her? Even after these untruths, they did not come easy to my lips.

But Uat entered Senet's sleeping room, rubbing her neck and brushing her hair back from her eyes.

"Do you need my help?" she asked. "I heard your concern. I do not know why I have so many headaches lately."

"I will call my physician. He will be able to solve this," Senet said.

Uat sighed. "Thank you. These headaches are becoming a problem for all of us."

As promised, Senet sent for her physician the next morning. Tiakken hurried to Senet's apartments with two assistants. He probed her, touching her forehead, taking her wrist in his hand, feeling her neck with the other.

"It is not me who is ill," Senet said, pushing Tiakken's hands away from her. "It is my servant, Uat. She has suffered from headaches lately. Many headaches. Can you find the cause?"

Tiakken turned to toward us, his gaze clouding. I gestured toward Uat. "Her."

Tiakken huffed and turned to Uat. He signaled to his second assistant to begin the same examination he had started on Senet.

While the assistant probed Uat's neck, felt her forehead, and pressed at her wrist, Tiakken spoke with Senet.

"Are you certain you are well? Do your womanly times still come regularly?"

Senet drew back. "What business is that of yours?"

"They end when you carry a child within you. Pharaoh asked that I care for you if that has happened."

"My healing woman is more than capable of caring for me when I become with child," Senet said, her voice cold.

"I am sorry," the physician stammered. "Pharaoh commanded me to ask."

"You can tell him his seed is not strong enough to give me a child yet."

Tiakken's eyebrows jerked toward his hairline. "I cannot tell Pharaoh that. He — he would have me killed right there. His seed has produced other children. Perhaps it is you."

Senet stiffened and glared at the physician. "Me? I hardly think so. I called you here to examine my servant, not to question my ability to have children. See to your task."

Tiakken turned and muttered to his assistant for a time. At last, he turned his attention back to Senet.

"This woman seems healthy. There is no obvious reason she should have headaches that keep her from your service."

Senet turned her glare on Uat.

"But I do have headaches," Uat whined.

"She does, Mistress," I said. "She rolls back and forth on her pallet with her head in her hands."

"And you have no potion to give my servant?" Senet asked in an imperious voice.

Tiakken dug into the bag at his waist and found a packet of powder. "Take this when you feel the headache coming on. It should stop it."

Uat took the packet and nodded.

Tiakken nodded to his assistants. "Is there anything else you desire from me?"

When Senet shook her head, he swept from the apartment.

Uat tucked the packet of powder into the bag at her waist. "I will have it here when I need it," she murmured.

Later, when Uat and I were alone, I turned on her. "This has gone on too long. I do not know what is taking you away from serving our mistress, but it must stop. She is suspicious. I cannot keep her from seeking you."

"I will not leave again," Uat promised, furrowing her brow.

She was true to her promise, and stayed with me, disappearing only for a short time when Pharaoh left Senet's apartment, then coming in to help in a rush.

"I am sorry," she told Senet. "I had to relieve myself."

Senet nodded and seated herself at her dressing table, waiting for us to help her get ready for bed.

Pharaoh visited Senet more often after that, but Uat did not disappear when he left.

Then one night after Senet slept, Uat left our room. I followed her quietly as she left Senet's apartment. I had to know why she left our room again.

At the intersection of halls, Pharaoh waited for her. He bent over and kissed her. Uat threw her arms around his neck and he lifted her into his arms.

"I missed you," he said.

"And I missed you," she replied.

I turned back to the apartment and our room. She had deceived me. *What would I tell Senet? Would I tell Senet? How could I?*

Removal

I watched Uat more closely after that. She disappeared in the night, returning near morning. She did not have the energy to laugh with Senet and me anymore. She had a sullenness when Senet spoke of Pharaoh.

I was torn. I knew Uat's problem. She desired to be with Pharaoh. She wanted to be his wife. However, she was the servant of his wife with little standing in the court. She could never be his wife.

This went on for weeks. Uat began to fall asleep at the pool when we washed Senet, and in the rooms when we dressed her hair and body. She rested on the floor, sagging into herself while I rubbed oils and ointments on Senet's body and feet.

I was not alone in noticing Uat's behavior. Senet quirked an eyebrow up as I massaged oil into her arms.

I shrugged. *How can I tell her of Uat's mutiny? She has treated me well, but Senet has a right to know. What can I do?*

When we were alone, I shook Uat. "You must stop leaving at night. I know where you go. Senet will learn of your treason."

"Where I go?" Uat feigned surprise. "I sleep here on my pallet, as you do."

"No. You leave almost every night. I watch you leave. You go to Pharaoh. You will pay for it."

Uat flipped her hair back. "He will protect me."

"Do you really think he can protect you from Senet's wrath?"

"He is Pharaoh."

"And what about me? I have kept your secret. When Senet discovers the cause of your inattention, she will be angry with me." Anger leaked into my voice, although I kept it soft.

"Why would she be angry with you? You sleep while I am gone. You do not know."

My jaw went hard as I clenched my teeth. "But I *do* know, and it is my responsibility to share it with Senet. You are making me ill." I tapped my foot and set my hands on my hips.

"Stop. It is not your problem. Pharaoh will protect me." She shook her head.

"Perhaps. But he will not protect me." My voice became sharp.

"You can be my servant when he marries me," she smirked.

I jabbed a finger at her. "Do you really believe Pharaoh will marry you? A nobody servant?" I narrowed my eyes.

"I am not a nobody. My family had money," she protested, stepping closer to me than I liked.

"No. They worked for money," I countered, stepping closer to her.. "They have no money and power now. If they did, you would not be Senet's servant, sneaking through the palace at night to be with Pharaoh," I growled. Something looked different about her. "Do you carry his child?"

Uat thrust out her chest and lifted her chin. "I do."

"Does he know?"

"Not yet."

I shook my head. "This will hurt Senet." I forced myself to be still while I wanted to shove her.

Uat yawned. "Do I care?"

"You should. She is good to you." I frowned at her without turning away.

Uat gawked at her slippered toes and scuffed at the floor. "I should care, I suppose, but I do not."

"You do not care about me, either," I said, my voice shaking.

"Why should I? You are just a poor girl from the riverbank," she snorted.

I turned away, determined to share with Senet what Uat had done.

"Uat," Senet said as we dressed her later that day.

Uat perched at her feet, doing little to help prepare her to go into the women's court to visit with the other women.

"Uat? Are you listening to me?"

Uat nodded but did not lift her head.

"Uat? Are you ill?" Senet spoke more sharply.

Uat lifted her head. "Sleepy."

"Do you not sleep at night?"

"Not much."

I paused behind Senet and watched Uat's face. She bit her lip and grimaced.

"Why do you not sleep at night? Night is time to sleep, not while you are to be serving me."

Uat's head popped up. "I cannot sleep."

"Why?"

I sucked in a breath. Would Uat give an honest answer? I should have told Senet long before now, but I did not want to hurt her. Now may be too late.

"I spend my nights in Pharaoh's bed. I get little sleep."

Senet drew back from Uat sharply. "You what?" She turned to me. "Did you know?"

My face burned with shame. "I found out only recently, but I should have told you. I did not want to hurt you."

"You did not want to hurt me? I would have thrown this little harlot from my rooms."

"And now?" Uat lifted her head and gazed at Senet. "What will you do now that I carry his child?"

Senet rose suddenly, her hands clenching and unclenching. She exploded, slapping Uat across the face. "You will leave the women's court. Now. You will leave the palace."

She stomped to the door and threw it open. "Yafeu! Come with your men!"

Stalking back into the room, she left the apartment door open.

"And you, Hagar." Her voice dropped dangerously. "You knew and you did not warn me. I can no longer trust you."

Breath escaped me and my muscles went weak.

Yafeu and three of his men rushed into the apartment. "You called, Senet?"

She pointed to Uat. "Take this fornicator out of the palace. Leave her on the edge of the city. She is never to be allowed inside the palace again."

"Let me get my possessions," Uat cried.

"Nothing is yours. I gave you everything, and you stole my husband," Senet raged, spittle dripping from her lips. "Take her now. I do not want to see her ever again."

"Pharaoh will have something to say about that," Uat cried, her nostrils flaring.

"He has no say in the women's court. You are my servant, and I say you go, never, ever to return." Senet pointed to the door. "Drag this useless piece of trash from my sight."

Yafeu nodded to two of his men who took Uat by the arms and dragged her screaming and shouting down the long corridor.

When we could no longer hear her cries, Senet turned to me.

"I will not have this woman as a servant any longer. She did not share with me her companion's treachery. I can no longer trust her."

I fell at Senet's feet. "I did not know what to do. I have never faced such base behavior. What was I to do?"

Her face remained rigid. "Your betrayal of my confidence in you is unforgivable."

I dropped my head and sobbed. "I wanted to tell you. I tried to tell you many times, but I could not force the words past my lips."

"And in this, you violated my trust. I cannot depend on you." Senet whispered in a hard voice. "What will you do when Pharaoh seeks to bed you?"

I gasped. "I would not. I could not!"

"It is Pharaoh. How can I trust you?"

I peered up at her. Tears flowed down her face.

"What will you have me do with her?" Yafeu asked. "Should I throw her from the palace as well?"

I gazed up at Senet. *Will I be dragged to the edge of the city and left to fend for myself? My parents! What will they do? Uat! You have ruined me.*

She slowly shook her head. "No. Find another lady who requires an attendant, a lowly lady."

"An Abram and his sister came to the palace this morning," Yafeu mused.

"And Pharaoh claimed the sister?" Senet spat.

Yafeu bowed his head. "You know the man better than me."

"What is her name?" Senet asked.

"Sarai."

"Give this woman, Hagar, to Sarai as her servant. Hagar will serve her well."

She did not send me from the palace! Part of me wanted to go back to my parents. But I knew I would never be accepted there again. No emotions filled me. I felt empty and heavy inside.

I had lived in the women's court of the palace. I enjoyed the baths and the food. I did not like the intrigue. Perhaps this Sarai would treat me kindly.

"Gather your possessions," Yafeu ordered.

"I apologize. I should have told you weeks ago of Uat's deceit." I bowed low before Senet, hoping she would change her mind.

"Leave my sight. Gather your belongings now and go. But leave your clothing. It belongs to me." Senet turned her back to me. "And Yafeu. I will need another servant."

"Another woman came to the court today. I will bring her to you," he said as I entered the room I had shared with Uat.

I quickly gathered my few possessions into a basket and returned to the room where Yafeu waited.

His man took me by the arm and pulled me out the door. It slammed behind me.

I shook his hand off my arm. "I will walk with you. You do not need to force me."

The man nodded and dropped his hand. He led me through the women's court into an area I had not been before. At a door, he stopped.

"This is where you are to stay. If this woman will not have you, you will be sent from the palace. Do your best to stay in her good graces."

He knocked on the door and tramped away. My heart pounded in my ears. *Will this woman accept me?*

I opened the door and stepped in to see an older woman. Her smooth skin shone. Her dark blond hair, lighter at the edges, gave the only hint she was not as young as Senet or me. Even the skin on her hands was without wrinkles. Her beauty shone through. No matter what her age.

A basket of clothing lay in front of her and she squatted on the floor with a colorful sleeping robe in her hands, tears leaking down her cheeks.

I could see why Pharaoh would want this woman, even older than Senet and Uat.

The woman wiped her eyes with the robe. "Who are you?" she demanded.

I dropped my eyes. Obviously, this woman was not expecting anyone to come serve her. "I am Hagar. Yafeu assigned me as your servant."

"Servant? Who did that?" she asked. "Why would I need a servant?"

"Every woman who comes to the women's court is given a servant. Yafeu assigned me to you," I said. The words tumbled from my mouth. If this woman did not accept me, what would I do? Would Mother and Father take me back? I took a deep breath and let it out.

"Senet sent me away from her apartments. She sent me here, hoping you would not have me." A tear dripped off my nose. I did not like the vulnerability I felt in this woman's presence.

She touched my arm. "I am grateful you came to help me. I left my servant with our other people."

"Thank you," I said through my tears and fell to my knees at her feet. " If you refused me, Yafeu will send me from the women's court and Pharaoh's palace. Do not send me away."

The woman knelt in front of me. "Why did Senet send you away?"

I glanced up into the woman's eyes and dropped them back to the floor. "I did not." I sniffed. "I did not ... warn her."

"Warn her? Of what?"

"Uat, the other girl who served Senet with me, lay with Pharaoh, Senet's husband. I did not share what I knew. Senet says I betrayed her trust. She says Pharaoh will want to bed me next."

"And you do not want that?" This woman's voice was impossibly kind and understanding.

"No, mistress. I want to find a man I can marry, if servants can do that. Only my husband will bed me."

The woman pulled me to my feet. "Hagar, I will not send you away unless you are unfaithful to me. I have information about me I want to remain confidential. Keep everything you learn about me to yourself. Share nothing you hear here with others. None of it. Only the unfaithfulness of sharing what you learn about me or from me will cause me to send you away."

I sobbed with relief. "Mistress, I will do everything you say. I will keep anything I learn of you to myself."

She patted my back. "Then we will get along. Call me Sarai."

I nodded.

"Will you help me put on my sleeping robe and take these loops from my hair?"

I had left my basket of possessions outside the door. With them were my squares of linen for wiping my nose. I wiped my nose on the back of my hand. Sarai handed me a square of cotton. "Use this."

I took it and blew my nose. Then I helped pull her sleeping robe over her head and pulled it straight. "This is a beautiful robe, but it is so ... so long."

"It is the way I like it," Sarai said.

I lifted my eyebrows. This woman was not from Memphis, or even Egypt.

"Sit in front of the mirror," I said. "I will help you with your hair."

Sarai rested on the stool in front of the dressing table in front of the polished brass mirror while I took the jeweled combs from her hair. I set each one on the table in front of her. "Are these beautiful combs yours?"

Sarai lifted one and examined it. "They are beautiful, but they are not mine. Ami and Sanura put them in my hair. I will need to find them and return the combs."

I brushed Sarai's hair with a stiff boar bristle brush I found on the table, pulling out the tangles and snarls the loops had caused.

"I will return them tomorrow for you, if you would like," I said.

"That would be lovely," she said with a sigh. "I am overwhelmed by all that has happened so suddenly."

My life changed suddenly again today as well. We will get along if we can learn to overcome these new challenges.

"The woman's courts are overwhelming," I agreed. "Will you want to sleep late in the morning?"

Sarai shook her head. It was strange to see her smile as she shook her head after her pensive thoughts. "No. I have a busy day tomorrow. Pharaoh has promised I can go see Abram tomorrow. He needs my tapestry to discuss the stars with Pharaoh."

Abram? She wants to see Abram, not Pharaoh?

"Who is this Abram?" I asked. I braided her hair.

"Abram is my ..." she paused and inhaled deeply. "He is my brother. He has done much for me. I love and miss him very much."

"It is good to love your brother." Nesu's face flashed through my remembrance. "I had a brother once, on the river." My hands fell still with the pain of the memory of his death.

"He did not know how to swim?" Sarai asked.

"He knew how to swim. He learned to swim early, although our mother never liked it. She feared the crocodiles. But Nesu loved the water ..." I chewed on the inside of my mouth, fighting the tears that wanted to race down my face. "But when a child fell into the river, he jumped in to retrieve her."

"Whose child was it? A sister?"

"No. Father and Nesu worked on a barge on the Aur, transporting grain up the river. Their employer brought along his little daughter for the day. She often rode on top of the load with few problems until they bumped into something in the middle of the river." I stopped to fight back the emotions.

Something. Grandfather Crocodile, most likely.

"She lost her balance and fell into the water. Nesu jumped in and pulled her out." The memory of him jumping into the river brought tears to my eyes. I scrubbed them away with my fists.

"Near the boat? Could he not climb back on the boat?" Sarai pressed her hand against her stomach.

"He pushed the girl back on the boat and Father reached to pull Nesu back on. But ..." I bit my lower lip, trying to control my tears. "A crocodile got him." I swallowed the pain of the memory. "Nesu's screams still haunt me. Father and the owner beat the crocodile with the long poles they used to propel the barge up and down the river. But the crocodile would not let go."

Sarai put her hand against her mouth, but it did not muffle her cries of pain for me. "That is worse than I expected it to be," she whimpered. "Did you see it?"

I ducked my head. "Yes. We gathered papyrus on the banks when their barge passed us." I closed my eyes and sucked in a breath, searching for control. "Nesu was older than me. He protected me from the bullies who lived near us and warned me about Pharaoh's men who hunted for young girls. After his ... his ... accident, his men found me and brought me here. Nesu was no longer here to protect me." I returned to braiding Sarai's hair for sleep.

"Your poor mother and father, to lose a son in that way, then to lose you to Pharaoh's household."

"It is not as bad for them to lose me. They know I live, for Senet sent them a bag of coins. Yafeu told me Pharaoh sends coins to them each month to pay for my service." I lifted a shoulder. "I suppose it is better for them and for me." I tied a string around the end of her braid to hold it in place.

"What do you get for your service?"

I gazed into the reflection of Sarai's eyes in the mirror. "Better food than I ever ate at home, nicer clothing than Father and Mother could buy or make for me, and a warm, dry bed to sleep in each night. I cannot complain. If Senet were to get her way and force Yafeu to put me out of the palace, my father and mother would lose their payment for my service. They lost Nesu's support when the ..." I swallowed the bile that suddenly filled my throat. "When the crocodile got him. I could not do that to my parents. I thank you for taking me in."

Sarai turned to me. "I will keep you with me as long as I am here, if you remember to keep everything you learn about me to yourself."

"Yes, mistress."

"It is Sarai. Do you have a place to sleep?"

"I am to be here to meet your needs at night," I said.

I wondered at the flash of concern that crossed Sarai's face. But she smoothed it. "Then we must find a place for you to sleep."

We walked together through her apartment. Hers was large, but not as large as Senet's. Pharaoh continued to honor Senet with her large apartment. We found a small side room near her sleeping room with a narrow pallet.

"This is for me," I told her. "These apartments were prepared to have a servant for the woman who occupies them."

"Then it is yours," Sarai said. Her eyes scanned at me. "Do you have possessions you need to gather and bring here?"

"They are outside the door." I strode to the door and retrieved my basket.

"That is not much," Sarai observed.

"Enough for me. I have no other clothing. Senet would not allow me to gather them. She says they belong to her." My hands hung loosely at my sides.

"If she refuses to allow you to recover them, I will get you more clothing."

Sarai's generosity and Senet's anger caused me to cry myself to sleep that night.

Sarai

Early the next morning, I took Sarai to the bathing room where I helped her bathe. She slipped a robe around her bare body before we returned to her apartment to dress and care for her hair.

I went to the kitchens to collect our morning meal while she went through her belongings. She insisted I join her at her table to eat.

"I do not like to eat alone. I have always had my ... my brother to eat with me," Sarai said, urging me to sit.

What was the hesitancy about calling Abram her brother? She did it before.

As we ate, she asked me to find places for her clothing while she was gone. She had a few baskets filled with clothing and other beautiful possessions. She did not want all the possessions removed from the baskets, hoping she could leave the palace soon. On the top of one basket was a tapestry.

After we ate, she unrolled the tapestry for me. "I wove this," she said, watching for my reaction.

"It is beautiful," I cried. White stars shone among a dark blue background. I remembered some from my nights with my family along the river. "And you wove it? I did not know great ladies worked like this."

"I am no great lady. We, Abram and I, and our servants, are herders. We have many sheep, goats, and cattle."

"Your wealth is in animals?"

"It is. We women use their wool to weave blankets, tapestries, and fabric for other items we need."

"You do it yourself?" I asked. "Mother, her friends, and I wove large sheets of papyrus to be used as sails and as writing material. I have never woven anything else." My thoughts returned to those days when our family had a peace we had not known before.

"What is papyrus?"

"It is a reed that grows along the shores of the Aur River. We strip off the outside parts and weave hats and baskets. The men bundle it to make river boats. We slice the inner parts of the plant to make the sails and writing material."

Sarai nodded. "Amazing. Perhaps you could show me how you do it sometime."

"If I can get some papyrus, I would love to show you. Your tapestry must have taken a long time to weave."

Sarai glowed at the compliment. "This is a special tapestry that I made it after we left Ur. Abram wanted to remember the stars overhead and asked me to make it for him. I will go sometime today to join Abram and Pharaoh with my tapestry. Abram will use it to teach him about the stars."

"It must have taken many hours to get these details," I said, fingering the stars. "And they are in place?"

Sarai took an edge and rolled the tapestry. "They are."

I helped roll the tapestry. "You will not leave this with Pharaoh?"

"No. It is mine. I will not give it up. He can look at it and Abram can use it to teach, but the tapestry is mine. I will not let it go to another."

"Not even your brother?" I asked.

"Especially not him. If I have it, Pharaoh will be forced to allow me to listen to their discussion."

I patted the rolled tapestry. "Smart."

"I try to be," Sarai said.

Sarai gave me instructions for her clothing and other possessions. She pulled a scroll of something much like papyrus from a basket and seated herself to read.

I looked at the scroll.

"What is this made of? It does not look like papyrus."

"My scroll?" Sarai held the scroll out and gazed at it. "This is made of vellum. It comes from the thin skin of a sheep. Not a reed."

"We use papyrus. Different."

"And you make it?"

"I did. Not anymore. Now I live here in the women's court." I closed my eyes and took a deep, cleansing breath. "Those were good days helping my mother and our friends make papyrus and weaving baskets to sell."

"You do not think you will return to that life?" Sarai asked.

"I doubt it. Few women leave the court, and if they do, they are driven out of Memphis." My shoulders drooped, thinking of Uat and her unborn child. Would they survive the desert? What would happen to them?

After I brought her food for our midday meal, a servant knocked on the door. He lifted the tapestry onto his shoulders and led Sarai from the room to direct her to where Pharaoh and Abram waited.

The door closed on Sarai and I stared at the room. I had not been left alone in the women's court before. I sucked in a long breath and returned to Sarai's baskets. I put some of her clothing in a chest but left most of her other possessions in the baskets and set them against the wall inside her clothing space.

With everything put away, I wandered through Sarai's rooms, searching for something to do. The jeweled pins sitting on her dressing table caught my eye. They needed to be returned to Ami and Sanura.

Senet had not interacted with Ami or Sanura. They were not the highest ladies in the court, but daughters of one of the other women. I did not know where to find them but considered the size of the court. How hard could it be?

Ha! I soon found out. I wandered through the women's court and found rooms and places I did not know existed, and still could not find these two young ladies. I poked my nose into rooms where I did not belong and was roundly chastised by the owners.

Finally, I asked Ketet.

"Ami and Sanura?" She tapped her lips as she thought. "They are down this passageway and to the left. Why do you need to find them?"

"My new mistress, Sarai, received these jeweled pins from them when she arrived here yesterday. She commanded me to return them."

"But those are hers. Did she not know they were for her to use?"

I shook my head and frowned. "It looks like she does not."

"Return them to your mistress, Sarai. She is to wear them here in the palace. Pharaoh wanted her to have them and other jewels he has gifted her. She is special to him."

I scratched at my temple. "I thought Senet was his wife."

"Senet is but one of Pharaoh's many wives. She is currently his favorite. He also has many concubines. I suspect he wants to marry this Sarai. They tell me she is quite beautiful, but I have not met her."

I allowed my lungs to expand as I breathed deeply. "She is beautiful, inside and out. She is kind to me in a way I never expected from a mistress."

Ketet held her face smooth. "No wonder Pharaoh is so interested in her. I heard she is older than his other wives."

I suddenly remembered the promise I made to Sarai. "She is a beautiful woman. I do not know her age, nor do I care. She is my mistress, and I do not share anything I learn in her apartments."

Ketet patted my arm. "That is as it should be. You should hurry back to her apartment with those pins. She will want to be dressed for the evening gathering."

"Thank you," I said, then turned on my heel to rush back to Sarai's apartment. I darted a glance at the passageways. "Which way is closest? I have not been here often."

Ketet pointed the way to Sarai's apartment. I scurried down the passageways and entered only moments before Sarai.

Sarai was surprised to learn that the jeweled pins were hers to keep. "Ami and Sanura did not tell me. I wonder why?"

"I suspect they assumed you would know. This is the way it is in the women's court."

Sarai squinted at me. "But you did not know either, Hagar. You should have told me, so I would not worry. You have lived here longer than I have."

I ducked my head. "I have only lived in the women's court for less than a year. Pharaoh's men brought me here against my wishes. It is good for my parents, so now I want to stay. I have only served one woman before you. Senet."

"Pharaoh's wife?"

"His current favorite wife. He has many." I repeated the information Ketet had given me.

"I do not plan to be one of his many wives," Sarai said, drawing herself tall and thrusting out her chest. "I do not plan to stay here in Memphis long."

"What brought you here?" I hoped to direct her attention from thoughts of Pharaoh.

"We escaped a drought in our homeland. We hoped to stay here until it ends."

I nodded. *Or until Pharaoh grows tired of you and allows you to leave.*

"Or sooner, if we can," Sarai whispered before she spoke louder to me. "Where do I go to meet these other women in this court?"

"The women gather in the socializing chamber in the late afternoon. They eat dinner together there."

"And you? Where do you eat?"

Sarai's concern surprised me. Senet never cared about my welfare. "I will sit along the edges of the chamber behind sheer curtains. I eat there. If you need anything, I will come to help you with it. All you need to do is lift your hand and flick your fingers toward me."

"Like this?" Sarai asked, lifting her hand and signaling.

"Yes. I will see that."

"That makes me feel better. I do not know my way around this big place yet." Sarai licked her lips. "I never lived in such a large place. And I was always mistress of my home. This is all new to me."

"You are an intelligent woman," I said, leaning forward. "You will learn this quickly. Shall I help you get ready for the gathering?"

Later, I escorted Sarai to the socializing chamber. I showed her where I would sit, then hurried to my place behind the curtains to watch her.

My heart stuttered as I watched her move into the room. She spoke to other women, but many responded with only a word or two and turned away. I wanted to go in and help her, but that was not my place.

Eventually, Sarai found a seat and lounged back, ignoring the other women. I waited for her to signal her need for me, but she never did. Servers brought her food. Then Nabukha joined her. I sighed in relief. Nabukha had been kind to me when I saw to Senet's needs.

I breathed out softly and stopped worrying about Sarai.

My eyes turned toward the center of the room and the women who surrounded Senet. As usual, it was difficult to see her. As Pharaoh's favorite wife, the others surrounded her, craving her attention. They could have it. I no longer desired it.

A new girl perched in the place where Uat and I once relaxed. Her elbows pressed into her sides as she shrunk into herself, trying to hide from the others. She wiped her hands on her shift over and over.

Poor girl. I remembered feeling the same way. She had probably been plucked from the streets the day before, as I was. I felt sorry for her, but as I had been forced to learn how to deal with these people, so would she.

If Sarai were part of those crowding Senet, I could approach the girl and offer her my friendship. But Senet did not offer to befriend Sarai. My responsibility was to care for Sarai, not befriend Senet's newest servant.

Slaves brought me a plate of food, which I picked at while I watched for Sarai's signal.

It never came. After eating and conversing with Nabukha for more than three hours, Sarai walked toward the exit. I hurried to join her.

We walked in silence to Sarai's apartments.

"I do like Nabukha. She is friendly, unlike many of the other women," Sarai said as I closed the door to her apartment.

"They believe Senet will help them rise. She will not. She likes their attention, but she wants it all. I lived with her for nearly a year. She never helped another woman. Not unless the other woman would help her. She is self-centered and vain. I see that now that I know you."

"She is Pharaoh's favorite. That gives her some rights."

"Not as many as she takes," I muttered.

"Will you say the same about me when I leave Memphis?" Sarai asked.

I turned to stare at her. "No. Never. I promised to keep everything about you to myself. I will do that if you leave Memphis." I crunched my eyebrows together. "Why would you ever want to leave Memphis?"

"I miss my home in Mamre. It is quiet there. We have no palace intrigues, no scheming queen."

I thought about my home. "I sometimes miss my home. It was quiet, too. We were not wealthy, with only a few coins to keep us living, but our family love made us wealthy ..." I bit my lip. "Until we lost Nesu."

HAGAR, MOTHER OF SORROWS

Sarai embraced me. "I miss my brother, too. We will keep on keeping on."

"Because we must," I agreed.

Sewing Circle

Over each of the next days, Sarai would receive a message warning her that a servant would come for her and her star tapestry shortly before the servant arrived. She always dressed carefully, as if planning to meet with her lover, rather than her brother and Pharaoh, who she insisted she would never marry. I found many ways to pin the jeweled pins in her lovely hair. She always smiled her thanks to me before leaving.

Sarai was not young, I knew that, but she glowed like a young woman going to meet her lover each time she left her apartment.

When Sarai returned, however, her smiles came with more difficulty. There was something, or someone, she missed when she returned.

At first, I checked to ensure the servant had returned her tapestry. I knew Pharaoh would never return it if he thought she had left it for him. But she always returned with her tapestry. She would return it to a place of honor in her room, touching it with a fondness not expected of a tapestry.

There was something she was not telling me. However, I was her servant. She was not mine. And if she had something she did not want to share with me, that was her right.

I found myself waiting for her return with a cup of wine. Often, Sarai would wrap me in her arms, holding the wine behind my back. She never cried, not in my presence, but her emotions were always near the surface after visiting her brother, Abram, and Pharaoh.

"Tell me about the way people here dress," she said one afternoon, after spending time with Abram and Pharaoh. "I see men and women whose clothing sweep across their sandals, and others whose clothing almost covers them. Why is that?"

I glanced down at my current shift, a bright blue given to me by Sarai. It reached almost to my knees, indicating my status as a servant to a great lady. I had been one who wore a shorter shift before coming to the women's court. I swallowed my embarrassment.

"The length of our clothing gives onlookers instant knowledge of our status. The very wealthy wear their kilts and dresses long enough to cover their feet. Anyone who sees them knows they are of wealth and will bow and scrape before them."

"Only the wealthy wear longer clothing?" Sarai asked and touched her chin.

"That is the way here in Memphis. Those who are naked, or nearly naked, are slaves. They have nothing of their own, not even their bodies. My shift is longer than some you will see here in the women's court. I am a servant, not a slave. And you, my mistress, are wealthy. The length of my shift demonstrates that honor."

Sarai tipped her head to the side. "So, all our herders and all our servants will be treated as wealthy men and women because we wear clothing that brushes the tops of our feet?"

My eyebrows shot up. "Even your servants wear clothing that long? You must be wealthy for everyone to wear clothing like that."

Sarai lifted a shoulder in a small shrug. "We cut the wool of the sheep and goats every year. Most we sell, but we keep some to spin into thread and weave into cloth to dress our bodies. I suppose that makes all of us wealthy."

"If we could wear papyrus, we could all be wealthy," I said. "I have made many things from all the parts of the plant, but never clothing."

"I saw boats and barges on the river. Did you not say these were made from papyrus?" At my nod, she continued, "It is a wonder plant."

Sarai moved to her sleeping room. "I am tired. I will rest for an hour. Wake me in time to prepare to join the other women at the gathering." She lay on her pallet and closed her eyes.

I went to her dressing room and found a lovely dress in her chest and some jewels to drape around her neck. She would be as beautiful as Senet this evening.

I noticed that none of her dresses showed her body the way Senet's dresses did. The neckline rose close to her neck, the sleeves came to her wrists, and the hems to her ankles. Yet, these dresses made her look appealing and stunning. She did not need to show her body as so many of our women did. No wonder Pharaoh was drawn to her.

"Do you sew?" Sarai asked one evening as we walked back from the socializing chamber.

"I learned to sew as a child. It was required if we wanted clothing to wear." My thoughts turned back to the days at Mother's knee as she showed me how to run stitches through the fabric to join them together. Later, she taught me how to make something beautiful from a simple piece of fabric.

"Nabukha and I have decided we are going to sew during the gathering. No need to sit back and be bored. After we eat, you and Nabukha's servant will join us."

I tipped my head to the side. "Why are you doing this? There is a reason beyond boredom."

Sarai grinned. "There is. We are tired of the queen bee thinking she controls everything. We plan to do something different — see what the other women do."

"But you plan to bring your servants close to sew with you?" I said with a gasp.

"We do. Is that a problem?"

"I have never been inside the socializing chamber unless I was called on to help my mistress, Senet." I rolled my lips inward. "You have never requested my help."

"I will request your help tomorrow. Be ready."

I did not know how Senet and the others would react to two servants sitting with our ladies in the socializing chamber. Would Senet become angry and insist Yafeu send us from the palace? The thought made me quiver.

"Do not fear," Sarai said as I opened our door. "It was Nabukha's idea, and she is Pharaoh's first wife."

I overcame my fear. If Nabukha insisted, we would be safe.

While Sarai waited for Pharaoh's servant to come for her the next morning, she dug through a basket I had not emptied. She found a colorful men's robe she had been sewing.

"It is for Abram," she said, pulling the robe close to her. "I am going to finish this."

She tucked the robe into a basket she had prepared to carry with her into the big room where the women gathered.

When Sarai and Nabukha signaled to me and Nabukha's servant, Heqet, we brought in their sewing baskets and perched on the floor next to them. Sarai and Nabukha pulled out their sewing and ignored the knot of women surrounding Senet. I worked to decorate a length of linen for a sash to wear around my shift. Heqet worked on a dress for herself.

A few of the women looked our way. It did not take long for one to wander over to ask what we did.

Sarai lifted the beautiful robe for all to see. Nabukha held up a dress. The women squealed with surprise, as though they did not know how clothing came to be. *Silly women.*

Some asked if Sarai and Nabukha would teach them. Nabukha smiled sweetly. "Certainly we will help you, if Senet gives you permission."

"We are our own women," one woman cried. "I will come prepared to learn tomorrow. What do I need?"

"What would you like to make?"

When she decided what she wanted, Nabukha gave her a list of materials she would need. The women watched us sew for a time, then drifted back to Senet, squealing and chattering about our work.

I ducked my head and continued to sew, but I Sarai and Nabukha giggled. Their plan would work.

Heqet and I left when the slaves served the food. We knew better than to stay among the great ladies while food was served. As we ate, the other servants came to us, asking what we did and how they could help their mistresses be prepared to learn from ours. For once, I was the center of attention for a good reason. My face felt stretched from all my smiles.

After the meal, Pharaoh came in, and as usual, went to speak with Nabukha and Sarai. He always spoke to Nabukha first, as she was his first wife, but I watched his eyes. They did not dwell on her. They focused on Sarai and her beauty. However, Sarai kept her head down, not looking up at Pharaoh or showing interest in him.

He said something, and she lifted the robe for Abram so he could see. She shook her head. His face fell and his shoulders drooped as he pouted. *He wanted that robe.*

Later, when we were back in her apartment, Sarai told me that Pharaoh thought the robe was for him.

"Silly man," Sarai laughed. "Not everything is for him. Definitely not this robe. I started it before we came here, and it is a special gift for Abram."

"I saw his face fall," I said.

"He said he would like some woman to care enough about him to sew something special for him. That woman is not me."

"Not you?" I asked. "I thought you were here because he wants you as his wife."

Sarai ducked her head and shook it. "I hope not. I do not want to live in Memphis for the rest of my life. I want to go back to Canaan."

"Can you do something to make him feel better?" I asked as I set my sewing basket on the floor near the door going toward my room.

"You are sewing a sash. Perhaps I could make a sash for him. We suggested Senet could make him something special, but ..." She lifted her hands as she shrugged.

"Senet!" I said, choking on the name. "No. She does nothing like that. She barely reads and writes."

"As I suspected. Nabukha did not believe she would even try to sew. We will have to see."

I shook my head and picked up our baskets. "I will put these away before I come to help you prepare for bed."

"No hurry," Sarai said. "I want to work on Abram's robe for a while longer."

The next morning, she asked me to get a length of linen to use as a sash for Pharaoh. "I will want black and red sewing thread for the design," she said. "I have a masculine pattern in mind that will look good on him."

While she went to meet with Abram and Pharaoh that afternoon, I went to the seamstress and asked for both a length of linen and black and red sewing thread.

"What is happening in the women's court?" the seamstress asked. "Many servants have come asking for linen and thread."

I lifted a shoulder. "I suppose the ladies want to sew."

I left her staring after me, unblinking. She had no fear. The women would tire of sewing soon enough.

Sarai cried in delight when she saw the linen and the thread. Before we left for the socializing chamber, she stitched the linen together and prepared it for the design she planned. She tucked it into her sewing basket with a skirt and pink and purple thread.

"I want this to be a surprise for Pharaoh," she explained. "He does not need to know until I complete the sash."

I carried her basket and mine to the socializing chamber. Rather than allowing me to move to my place on the edge of the room, she tucked her arm in mine and led me to her place in the room. Nabukha and Heqet were there already, sewing.

I withdrew my sash and began to sew. Sarai pulled out the sash she planned to make for Pharaoh.

Nabukha shook her head. "You are really going to sew him something?"

"He is a good man. He is lonely," Sarai said.

"Lonely!" Nabukha almost choked on the word. "Not him. He has people surrounding him all the time. He is never alone."

"But no one loves him. I have never seen his mother," Sarai insisted.

"No. His mother died last year. I suppose he is lonely. My mother is gone, as well."

"So is mine. I miss her."

Nabukha set a hand on her arm. "You are a strong woman."

I caught Sarai peering up at Nabukha, a question on her face. But she said nothing to her friend.

I missed my mother's love. I would never see her again. In some ways, it would be easier to think of her as dead.

Sarai shook her head. "I wish to be stronger."

Two women left Senet's circle that day and joined us. Each had a dress to sew designs on. Nabukha and Sarai sat next to them and patiently showed them where to put the needle each time. My skin tingled as I watched them working with the women who had spent so much time with Senet.

Sarai and Nabukha treated them well, smiling with them over their successes and helping them resolve their problems.

As we had the day before, Heqet and I returned to our place along the wall when the slaves served meals.

"Can you believe how generous Nabukha and Sarai were with their time?" Heqet asked with her eyes wide open. "After the way those women treat our mistresses, I do not understand why they would be so kind."

"Because our mistresses are not like Senet," I said. "Senet will not like that her little group of women slip away to work with Sarai and Nabukha."

"Nabukha laughed and laughed the night she came home with the idea of sewing here. She said poor Senet would not know what happened to her knot of admirers when they desert her for us."

"Only two, so far," I said.

"There will be more. I saw them glancing at us with longing eyes. Perhaps even Senet will join us," Heqet said with a laugh.

"Not Senet. She has never done anything with her hands. I had to tie her dress and shoes when I worked for her."

"I thought I had seen you over there earlier. What happened?"

Before I was forced to share my embarrassment, Pharaoh strode into the room toward our mistresses. Sarai had traded the sash for her skirt before he entered. I saw her hold it up and his eyebrows rise. Her ruse was working.

Sarai spoke with him as much as Nabukha that day. Pharaoh's eyes jerked from Sarai toward the women crowding around Senet. His face had reddened and his head lifted. He threw his shoulders back and tramped toward Senet, giving her followers time to move from his way before he barged past them.

Before long, he escorted Senet from the socializing chamber with a broad grin on his face.

"What did you say to Pharaoh that made him rush over to Senet?" I asked when we were alone in her apartment once more.

"I asked if he saw Senet's belly. It grows."

"Senet will give Pharaoh a child? It must have happened before she kicked me out," I said. Excitement tickled my stomach.

"Perhaps then, or shortly after. I doubt she knew of the child for certain yet. She will soon. She has a glow about her."

I drew my head back and my eyebrows close together. "A glow?"

"Look for it tomorrow. Women who carry a child within them have a glow. You can see it if you look for it." Sarai put her sewing basket away and stretched her back. "It has been a long day."

"If Senet is with child, Pharaoh will stop bothering you, at least for a time." I massaged Sarai's shoulders. She breathed a soft sigh and relaxed.

"For a time. I hope to be gone from this place before he changes his mind."

"What will get you away from Memphis? Do you not love it here?"

"I would love it more if I were with Abram and our people. I do not like to be separated from them," Sarai said with a frown. "Besides, although the river is lovely, it causes my hair to fly away. I always feel wet."

"The moisture keeps our skin lovely."

"Perhaps, but I miss the desert."

"It would be difficult to live in a land with no water," I said, imagining tall dunes of sand and a dearth of trees and vegetation.

"The desert is a lovely place. We know where and how to find water. Our desert is not like the desert surrounding Egypt. We have trees and flowers to cool and beautify our homes."

"It is not dry and desolate?" I asked in a soft, shaky voice, hoping never to learn.

Sarai chuckled softly. "No. Nothing like that. There are places with little water, but the land supports plants and animals. It supports us and our herds. It could not be desolate."

"I had not considered that. How many animals do you have?"

"We have many hundreds between Abram and Lot, our nephew. Our animals make us a wealthy people."

"You do not carry gold or silver with you?"

Sarai smiled and shook her head softly. "Why would we do that? Our wealth trots behind us on their four legs. Gold and jewels are heavy. We have little of it."

The next day, when Sarai returned from her daily visit with Pharaoh and Abram, she plopped heavily in her seat. "You will never believe what Pharaoh has done."

"What did he do this time?" I asked as a pit opened up in my stomach.

"He gave us oxen as a gift." Her eyes widened. "I had not expected a gift. All I did was tell him to ask Senet about the babe. He did all that was necessary to put the child in her belly. I had nothing to do with it."

"But you told him about it. He will connect you to the child. I hope it is a boy child."

"As do I," Sarai muttered. "Perhaps now he will give up on marrying me and allow me to leave his court."

"Perhaps. I have not lived here in the court much longer than you. I do not know how capricious the man is. I heard stories when I lived with my parents, but I do not know how true they were." For Sarai, I hoped he would.

"I will finish the design on the sash and give it to him. Perhaps that will encourage him to let me leave." She pulled the sash from her workbasket and sewed on it until time to go to the socializing chamber.

The group of women who joined Sarai and Nabukha had grown. Even the young woman who now served Senet joined us.

"I have been instructed to learn to sew so that I may teach my mistress," she whispered to me. "I have sewn for much of my life, but Senet does not know. This gives me an opportunity to be with other women during the social time."

87

"I will not share your secret," I mumbled. "Pretend to need help for a day or two."

"I planned to," the young woman whispered.

Each day we sewed together in an ever-growing circle of women until time to eat. Then the women would desert Nabukha and Sarai for Senet.

On the day Sarai completed the sash for Pharaoh, I watched when he entered the women's quarters. As usual, he walked directly to Nabukha and Sarai. Nabukha still deserved the honor of his first visit.

Sarai lifted the beautiful sash from her basket. I could see her speaking to him but could not understand the words. She handed the sash to him with a bow.

Pharaoh fingered the sash, then lifted it to his forehead with a grin, then draped it over his shoulder. Then, after exchanging a few words, he bent and kissed Sarai on the cheek.

After more words between them, he tipped his head back and laughed before swaggering over to show Senet.

As we seated ourselves the next afternoon, Senet hurried to join us. Although I wanted to draw away from her presence, Sarai's presence steadied me. "How did you make that ... sash for Pharaoh? Will you teach me?"

Sarai asked if she had the needed materials. Senet's face fell until she remembered. "I will ask Yafeu to bring me what I need. Then will you teach me?"

"Request a sharp needle as well," Nabukha suggested, showing her needle to Senet. "You cannot sew without a needle."

Senet waited for us the next afternoon with her sewing supplies. Sounding like a giggling girl, she listened to Sarai's and Nabukha's instructions. I expected her fingers to struggle with the new skill, but she learned faster than the others in her group.

Most afternoons after that, Senet's circle of women joined us. I expected to be sent away, since I was a servant. However, even Senet's servant was allowed to stay during the sewing time.

Even after Senet became confident, she found reasons to sit with us and share the gossip of the palace.

Departure

A nd then one afternoon, Senet did not join us.

Nabukha asked the women who usually surrounded Senet why she had not joined us.

"Have you not heard?" one lady replied. "She is ill and has taken to her bed."

"The child?" Sarai gasped.

"Is still within her, but ..."

I sucked in a breath as Sarai asked how long she had been ill.

"Since last night."

"Is a healer with her?" Nabukha asked.

"He is, but he fears for the child," the woman said, tears falling across her face and onto her sewing.

Sarai hurried away from the group of sobbing women back to her apartment. I followed her and watched as she closed the door behind her. I heard her sobs and silently turned the latch and entered her room.

Sarai knelt in the middle of the room with her hands held above her head, begging someone she called Jehovah to save Senet's baby. She cried she did not want to see another suffer as she had suffered. I remained next to her, silently repeating her words, even as they made little sense to me. Although I did not understand, I trusted Sarai.

She looked up at me.

"You are one of those?" I asked, rubbing my forehead.

"One of what?" she asked.

"One of the Jehovah cult."

Sarai blew out her breath. "It is not a cult, but yes, I worship Jehovah. He is my God and the God of my people from the beginning of time. He has protected me many times. His blessings have been abundant."

"Can this Jehovah save Senet's baby?" I asked, sucking in a breath and holding it.

Sarai stared into my eyes, searching deep into my heart, before she answered. "He can, if He chooses to bless Senet and Pharaoh in that way."

Air escaped in a rush. "Then I will join you in your prayers. Elkenah cannot save the child's life, or anyone else's. That so-called god only takes the lives of our children."

Sarai nodded.

I moved to my knees, ensuring my feet rested against the door. I did not want others to enter during our prayers. None in the household needed to know of our worship.

We remained still after our prayers, each of us thinking. It had been almost two hours when Yafeu pounded on the door.

I flicked a glance at Sarai before opening the door. She sat with her shoulders back and her head up, prepared for whatever would come next.

Yafeu barged into the room with three male bearers. "Pharaoh demands you leave immediately."

Leave? To visit Abram and Pharaoh?

Sarai smiled gently. "Does he desire me to come meet with him and Abram this late?"

Yafeu stomped a foot. "No. You and your husband are to leave Memphis. Gather your things and go now."

"Your husband?" I whispered.

"Husband? Who is —"

"We know you are married to Abram. He admitted it to Pharaoh. These men are here to carry your possessions," Yafeu barked.

No wonder her face went soft when she spoke of Abram. But what will I do? Who will I serve if Sarai leaves? Life has been good since I became her servant. Now what?

"May I have the time necessary to repack my possessions?" she asked. "It should not take long."

Yafeu brought his hand down sharply. "A very short time."

I leapt to my feet to help her.

"Hagar. You must gather your possessions as well," Yafeu ordered. "Pharaoh has given you as a handmaid to this woman. You will leave with her."

"Leave the women's quarters?" I gasped. "This is my home!" *Where would we go? Into the desert?*

"It was your home. No longer. Your home is wherever Abram and Sarai take you."

My stomach fluttered as I stepped back. He could have given me less pain if he had slapped me across the face.

I glanced from Yafeu's flinty face to Sarai's excitement and sucked in a deep breath. I rushed to the little room I had occupied since the evening Yafeu brought me here. I quickly gathered my few possessions.

What had I done to be given to Sarai? Why would Pharaoh send me from my homeland, away from Memphis, the Aur River, the crocodiles, and my parents? Would I ever see them again? Mother! I am sorry you will no longer receive coins for my service. What will I do? How will I survive away from the river? Away from the women's court? Away from my parents?

I set my basket beside my door, then I went to help pack Sarai's clothing and her other belongings.

"What about these jeweled combs?" she asked, holding out the combs put in her hair the day she came to the women's quarters. "I thought you were going to return them to Ami and Sanura."

"I took them to her. Ami said they are yours, a gift from Pharaoh."

She carried them to Yafeu. "Do you want these back?"

He took the combs in his hands, turning them over. "No. Pharaoh gave these to you. They are yours. Put them in your baskets and take them with you. Are you ready to go yet?"

"Soon," she said.

We checked the clothing space to ensure we left nothing behind. I carried her baskets and bags into the sitting room.

"I am ready," Sarai said.

I brought my basket in, ducking my head, not wanting to say anything.

Yafeu growled at me. "Is this everything?"

"Yes. I am ready to go. Are you certain Pharaoh gave me to Sarai?"

His frown told me I should not ask. *It had happened. I belonged to Sarai, body and soul. I no longer owned my soul. I am no longer free. I had no freedom since Pharaoh's men brought me to the women's court. I could not leave the women's court before. Now he was expelling me and sending me into a strange land.*

"Follow me," Yafeu said, then strode down the familiar corridors and out of the women's quarters.

I paused at the door and gazed back. "I had a good life here." I forced the tears that wanted to flow to the inside of my mouth. Yafeu did not need to see my grief.

Sarai touched my arm gently. "I hope you find life with us to be as good. We are good people."

On the steps outside the palace, a man dressed in long, light-colored robes waited. Sarai fell into his arms. He kissed her and held her close.

"I missed you," Sarai said.

"And I missed you," Abram replied.

"How did Pharaoh find out about us?"

"He said an angel warned him he could not take you as his wife, for you were mine. If he did not return you to me, his household would be plagued until he did."

"He will not kill you to keep me?" Sarai said. Her words were colored with the tears I held back, except hers were joyful. Mine were filled with sorrow.

"No. We are friends. We had too many fruitful discussions about the stars, planets, and numbers. He will not kill me. But because we deceived him, we are not allowed to stay within the boundaries of his lands. He commanded us to leave."

"He gave Hagar to me as a handmaid. His anger must not be terrible."

I frowned. A gift for anger?

"He gave men to me as servants as well. He begged me not to call more disasters onto his house. His fathers once worshiped Jehovah even when they could not use the Priesthood of God. He asked that I pray for his favorite wife, Senet."

We did that, too. May it bless her.

"Hagar and I prayed for her this afternoon. Is she healed yet?" Sarai asked.

I leaned close, listening for Abram's answer.

"It is in Jehovah's hands. I prayed for Senet and her child when I heard of her illness. Pharaoh has been good to us. He deserves this child. It will be a boy."

Yafeu waved at us, encouraging us to leave. We walked down the stairs, followed by the three bearers who carried our baskets and bags. Abram led the way toward the gate, where we met Abram's herders.

A woman separated from the crowd and embraced Sarai. "We missed you."

"And I missed you, Bara. This is Hagar, my new handmaid. Can you help her?"

Bara led me into the mass of people toward the other women. A man held the nose of a camel kneeling in the sand. I shuddered at the sight. This animal was larger than Grandfather Crocodile. She showed me how to sit on a camel, then mounted hers.

I twisted my neck to see where the bearers put mine and Sarai's possessions. They set them in a cart, then took up a place among the other servants. These men, too, were now part of Abram's and Sarai's household.

As we passed through the gate of Memphis, I settled onto the wide seat atop the camel and gazed along the river, wondering if I would see my parents. Would Father be one of the many barges floating down or being pushed up the Aur? Was Mother in the papyrus islands, cutting papyrus for more baskets and sails?

"I will always remember you," I whispered.

I clung to the saddle horn in front of me until at last I adjusted to the sway of the camel's stride. There is little like the sway of a tall camel. After I learned to balance astride him and hold on to the saddle horn, I relaxed enough to view Egypt and set it firmly into my memory.

Three young men separated from the caravan and ran toward the river, in the direction of my parent's home.

"Where are they going?" I asked Bara.

"I do not know. We will ask when they return."

Before we had traveled far, the young men returned, reported to Abram, and joined the other herders. I wanted to rush over and question them, but Bara held me back.

"We will have time to learn of their mission when we stop for the night."

Even though I rode atop a tall camel, dirt and dust stirred up from all the animals, getting in my clothes, on my face and in my eyes. I could not wipe away the dust. My eyes ran. I could imagine the muddy trails left on my face, and it made me cry even more.

The only thing that helped me survive the dust and dirt was the desire to know why the three young men had run off towards my parents' home.

The camels finally stopped, and a boy urged mine to kneel so I could climb off. I could almost move after sitting astride it all day. I limped from the camel with Bara. She had me sit on a rock while the others set up tents and prepared the evening meal.

Sarai found me. "How are you surviving the ride?"

I groaned. "Not well. I never thought riding on a camel would hurt."

Sarai nodded. "It is difficult to do when you first do it. Your body will soon learn to ride."

"I hope so." Tears slid down my cheeks.

Sarai's arms enfolded me, reminding me of Mother. I set my head on her shoulder and sobbed. "I did not expect to leave the palace today. I hoped to slip away from the women's quarters one day to visit Mother and Father. Now that will not happen. They will never see me again and will never learn what happened to me."

"We can send\ a letter to them, tell them you are with us," Sarai suggested.

"We could," I sniffed, "But neither Mother nor Father read."

"No one there reads?"

"No," I shook my head. "I could not read until I went to the palace."

Abram touched my shoulder. "I know they depend on the help Pharaoh sent them."

I sucked in a deep breath. "They do. How will they survive without that income?"

"I sent men to take coins to your parents. My messengers told them you will not return and there will be no more coins. I hope they use them with care."

"You sent coins to my parents?"

Abram nodded his head.

I threw my arms around Abram. "Thank you," I sobbed.

When my tears stopped, Bara led me away from Sarai and Abram to the tent set up for servants. As we entered the tent, I peeked back at Sarai, worrying she would require my help.

"Do not worry," Bara said. "Sarai and Abram will be fine without your help. You can help her tomorrow morning. She needs to be alone with her husband now. They have been apart for much too long."

I chewed on the inside of my mouth. "Are you certain?"

"I am certain." The tent door dropped behind Abram.

"Come with me," Bara said, touching my arm.

I followed her to sit beside a campfire. A woman dished up a bowl of soup and handed it to me. Another woman handed me a spoon. It tasted better than any of the sweetmeats I had eaten in the women's quarters.

The three young men who had run from the caravan found me as I leaned back to listen to the people milling about.

"We found your parents," one said.

"Tall man, strong arms, broad shoulders, dark hair, green eyes, works on the river?" I asked.

They nodded.

"The woman, shorter, but still tall. Light brown hair, dark eyes?" My gaze darted from one man to the other.

"Tabia's eyes were like yours, and Erfan's face was the same shape as yours," one young man said.

I inhaled a sharp breath.

"Her hair was lighter than yours, but I could tell she was your mother. They both wept when we told them where you had been and where you were going."

"Your father did not want to take the coins Abram sent. He only wanted you to return. But since that is not possible, your mother agreed to take the coins. They wished you a happy life with us."

I rolled my lips inward, seeking to prevent tears from falling across my face. It did not work. They fell anyway.

"Your parents are healthy and well, and your baby brother is beautiful," one of the young men said.

"Baby brother? I have a baby brother?" Joy contended with my grief. I would never see him.

When they nodded, the tears became sobs. "I will never see him. But he is there to take mine and Nesu's place. They will be happy without me."

I had always hoped to return to my home, if only for a brief visit. Now that was gone. It would never happen. My heart ached at the loss of family and the future I had longed for.

Moreh

That first night of the journey passed quickly. Pharaoh's guards rattled their staffs against our tents, waking everyone. I woke with a start, staring wildly at the tent.

"You must be on your way," the leader said. "Pharaoh wants you out of his land today."

Oh yes. We were expelled from Egypt.

We scurried to dress and prepare to leave. Men rolled our beds and took down the tents, strapping them all onto camels and donkeys.

When Abram and Sarai mounted their camels, the people sang songs of joy as we moved away from my beloved parents on the Black River and the city of Memphis. I did not sing, but I listened to their joy. They were happy to return to their home while I grieved to leave mine.

I wondered what the other servants Pharaoh had given to Abram were thinking and feeling. I determined to find them and learn. They were my countrymen and women. I could offer them solace. Truthfully, I desired solace in their company.

I stayed busy each evening, cooking and preparing for the next day's travel. I attended to Sarai's needs each morning and evening before Abram closed the door to their tent.

Each evening before I returned to my tent and the women who were becoming friends, I walked through the camp. I sought the familiar faces of Egyptian men and women wearing Egyptian clothing.

But I saw none. Like me, they had adopted the dress of Abram's people.

I found one bearer.

"I am busy caring for the baggage and doing as required, as you should be," he said shortly.

"You do not mind traveling with these people?" I asked.

"They are good to us, as they are good to you. Be grateful they took us in." He turned his back on me and lifted a heavy tent from off a camel. "I have work to do."

I was alone in the camp. No others from Egypt to share my sorrow.

I found my way back to Bara and the other women, who gladly accepted me. Time to become like them, happy to travel north into a new land.

What would I see? What would happen to me?

We moved slowly, for there were many animals to herd along the trail. We stopped many times, waiting for a herder to help a ewe deliver a lamb or a nanny to deliver a goat. Then we moved onward. I saw the herders carrying tiny sheep and goats in slings across their shoulders for the day. By the next morning, the little ones could keep up with their mothers.

I watched the others pray each morning and evening to Jehovah. They allowed me to sit nearby without joining in the prayers. They did other things that made me curious about Jehovah.

Then, after traveling many weeks, we stopped in the middle of the day. Servant men set up tents and Abram walked through the sheep, choosing young rams.

"What is Abram doing?" I asked Sarai.

"Searching for perfect lambs," she said.

"Why?"

"We are here in Sichem to offer sacrifices to Jehovah in gratitude for our protection."

I stared at the sheep. "You offer sheep to Jehovah? The priests of Elkenah offer bulls. The priests of Sobek offer antelope. Sometimes they both offer children and virgins."

"I know," Sarai said, turning to me. "We have experienced sacrifices to Elkenah. It was not something I want to do again."

"Experience? Not observed?" My heart raced at the thought.

"In Ur," Sarai said.

I waited, but she did not continue. It must have been horrible. *How can one experience a sacrifice and live?* I shuddered.

I watched with the others as Abram offered the sacrificial lambs to Jehovah, retaining a portion of the meat for all the congregation to eat afterward. When he lit the fire to burn the portion of the lambs for Jehovah, my jaw dropped. This was nothing like anything I had observed on feast days when the priests of Elkenah and Sobek offered sacrifice. Rather than horror and disgust, a warmth filled me.

Surprise caused my stomach to flutter. How could a sacrifice make me feel good? I was determined to ask Sarai about it when I could.

We celebrated that day, then the day after we packed our tents and continued to travel north.

I had expected dry sand dunes, but the land held flowers and trees. Green grass filled many of the valleys we passed through. Sarai had told me of the beauty of this land, but I had not believed her then. Now I did. The hills were rocky, but grass grew among the rocks. The sheep and goats wanted to skip away into the hills to feed on the green grass. I watched the herders work to keep them jogging down the path.

Eventually, a cheer lifted through the caravan. I looked at Nitza, who served Sarai's niece, Galya. "What is it? Are we safe?"

She turned to me with wide, glowing eyes. "Home. We are home."

I gazed at the pattern of rocks that outlined paths. "Home? This is your home? Where are the houses? Does Abram have a palace?"

She giggled. "No. We are herders. We live in tents."

Tents? I had hoped to see comfortable buildings, not an open valley. I frowned at the joyous people. How could they be so happy to live in tents!

The men put up the tents we had used on our journey, setting a smaller one for me near Sarai's and Abram's tent. One of the young men found my basket of belongings and brought it to the tent. They also brought the bedding I had slept in all the time we had traveled. Bara had given me beautiful blankets.

I stepped into the tent, stopped, and turned in a slow circle. The tent was small, but I had never had a space of my own before. I had always shared with someone, except the tiny room beside Sarai's in the women's court. This tent was spacious.

After I put things away, I went to see if Sarai needed help. Abram had left to help take the animals out to give them water.

Sarai reclined in a chair in front of her tent with baskets surrounding her. Some were open, with things spilling out. Men had moved some trunks inside and set them near the walls of the tent.

"May I help you?" I asked.

"It feels so good to be home," she said. "Could you help put things away?"

I opened the nearest basket and put their possessions in trunks as she directed. Soon I had everything settled as well as if we lived in an apartment in the women's court.

We walked outside together and she showed me the land she loved, pointing out the paths to each person's home tent and the places she found important. We watched the animals come in from the hills and the well.

The land was beautiful. Abram set up their tent near a tree where we could sit out of the heat.

I could enjoy a place like this.

Often, over the next few weeks, when I went out to watch the animals come in from the hills, Abram's men and Lot's men were arguing. I heard them shouting at each other.

"You drove your sheep into the field where I planned to feed our sheep," one of Lot's men shouted.

"You know we always feed our sheep in that field," Abram's herder shouted back. "You have no reason to believe you can feed your sheep there."

The men raised their fists, threatening each other.

I stepped back behind the nearest tent and shuddered while I waited for the shouting ended. I had not often heard men shout like that without coming to blows. I returned to the cooking fire between Sarai's and my tent where we had a lamb stew cooking over a fire. I had cooked for my mother, but never over an outdoor fire until we came on the journey here. I learned to cook as they did. Sarai's previous maid, Yael, and Bara were excellent teachers.

One herder, Danil, came to speak to Abram. Sarai took her spindle outside and seated herself near the tent to listen in as she spun. I wanted to listen too, but it was not my problem. Instead, I spun yarn on my spindle, preparing it to weave.

When Danil left, Sarai gestured for me to join her and Abram.

"I never thought having large herds would cause problems. We should invite Lot and Galya over for dinner to discuss this," Abram said, shaking his head.

"Hagar, would you please go extend an invitation to Lot and Galya to join us to eat this evening?" Sara asked.

I set my spinning on a chair and walked to Lot's tent. I scratched at the tent door. When no one came out, I walked to the side of the tent. Galya stood with a young child on her hip, stirring a stew.

"Sarai and Abram would like you to come join them for the evening meal tonight," I said.

Galya glanced at Lot.

"We were just speaking about inviting them," Lot said. "We will be happy to join them."

"I will let them know," I said.

"It is good you are there to help Sarai, Hagar," Galya said. "She has always had a maid."

"Pharaoh gave me to her," I said.

Galya inhaled sharply. "He gave you to Sarai? How did that happen?"

I shrugged. "Pharaoh's men took me from the street as I went to get water for my mother one day. They took me to Senet to serve her. When she no longer wanted me, I was taken to Sarai to be her maidservant." I lifted my hands upward. "When Pharaoh learned Abram and Sarai were married, he sent me along as her maid. I suppose he did not know I was once a free citizen. But young women are always at risk if his men find them on the streets."

"That is horrible," Galya replied in a squeak. "You should be home with your parents, Hagar, finding a man to marry, not here as Sarai's maidservant."

"It is done. Abram paid my parents for my service. I am here and it cannot be changed." I shook my head. "I am happy with Sarai. But now I must return and help finish the meal. We will see you soon?"

Galya nodded as I turned on my heel to hurry back to help Sarai.

When I returned to Sarai and Abram, I shared that Lot and Galya had been about to invite them.

"Lot is seeing the same problems," Abram murmured.

"It is a good thing I planned a larger meal for tonight," I said, and moved to the fire to complete the meal.

Sarai followed me. "Would you like me to help with something?"

I wrinkled my forehead. "No, mistress. I want to show you how much I have learned. I did not know I could cook for others or help a lady like you when they took me to the women's court."

"You learned fast."

My face warmed from her praise. "I appreciate the opportunity to learn, and the space to be alone. I have never had that before."

"You are welcome to it here. You are a great help to me. If you change your mind —"

"I will call you."

She returned to her tent and I returned to my cooking. When I slipped in to set dishes on the table, she had already placed a lovely cloth and special dishes on it. We would be ready when Lot and his family arrived.

Lot, Galya, and their little daughter arrived and when they were all seated at the table, I served them. When they heaped praises on my cooking efforts, I ducked my head, then lifted it to thank them for the praise.

During their meal and after, while they discussed their problems, I walked out into the night, working my spindle as I gazed into the night sky. My hands stilled. The stars shone brightly here, brighter than I had ever seen them in Memphis.

I remembered Sarai's woven tapestry. It matched these bright stars. No wonder Pharaoh wanted to keep it.

I heard Abram and Lot come out of the tent. I knew their men were arguing and wondering what they would do to solve the problem. But, it was not my problem. I returned to the cooking fire to put the food away and clean up the dirty dishes. Abram and Lot passed where I worked.

"Choose," Abram said. "If you go left, I will go right. If you choose right, I will go left. Which direction will you take?"

They walked on past me and their voices dimmed. Either way would mean we would leave this lovely valley and finding a new home. It saddened me to think I would not see Galya and some of the other women who befriended me when I joined them. These women were more friendly than any who lived in Pharaoh's women's court.

I sighed. I had no say or choice in any of this. It did not matter to me if Lot chose the left or the right. Pharaoh had given me to be Sarai's maid servant.

The men walked back toward me. "It will be as you request," Abram said, taking Lot by the hand. "I will move to the west. You move to the east. I will miss you."

"And I will miss you, Uncle." Lot threw his arms around Abram. I had not experienced family love like this. Our family had never shown affection openly. It surprised me.

From the other side, I overheard Galya speaking to Sarai. "I will miss you. You have been more than an auntie to me. You have been more like my mother."

Sarai cared for everyone. In many ways, she cared for me much as my mother had.

"Come back to see us," Sarai said in a choked voice.

It happened faster than I expected. Word spread among all the residents of Moreh to pack their possessions to travel once more soon after Lot and Abram separated. The next morning, we all woke early and loaded our belongings back onto the backs of camels and donkeys.

I embraced those women who had befriended me and would leave with Lot and Galya. I had lost too many friends, too many good people. I mourned their loss. However, I mounted my camel and followed Abram and Sarai as they turned west toward Canaan.

Conversion

We rode for three days before reaching the plain of Mamre. The men set up our tents, then Abram took Danil to gather stones and build an altar.

Once more, Abram walked through the herds of sheep, taking out pure white male lambs. I wanted to ask questions about the sacrifice this time, so when Abram prepared for the sacrifice, I made my way to the front to sit next to Sarai.

As we watched, she shared with me the purpose and meaning of each of Abram's movements. I asked questions and she answered without complaint.

"Your Jehovah protects you?" I asked.

"He kept me safe from Pharaoh in his palace. He never tried to bed me."

"That is true. I wondered how you avoided that. I heard of other women who came to the court and accepted Pharaoh's invitation to bed with him."

"Jehovah protected me as He protected Abram."

I wondered often if Senet had given birth to her child. Since we left, my distrust of her had softened. "Have you heard anything from Memphis? Did Senet and her child survive?"

"A trader we passed yesterday told us that Senet gave birth to a healthy baby boy in the spring."

"Jehovah be praised," I said. "I know we prayed for her. I did not know Jehovah could heal her and keep her safe."

"He did."

We watched Abram complete the sacrifice. Once more, his actions did not horrify me as the sacrifices of Elkenah's or Sobek's priests. I detested it when they took the lives of little children. When Abram took the life of an unspotted male sheep, I felt warm inside, rather than disgusted.

Sarai rode with me part of the time as we traveled the next three days. "You have lived among our people all this time," she said. "Are you ready to learn more about what we believe?"

I glanced down at my camel's neck and pushed the hair from my face. "You and your people seem to believe in Jehovah."

"We do believe. We have seen Jehovah's hand in our lives. He has protected us from sacrifice."

I lifted my eyebrows. "Oh?"

"When we still lived in Ur, the priests of Elkenah decided they needed a sacrifice. They had already sacrificed three of the daughters of Onitah, descended directly from Ham."

"Our Pharaohs came from Ham."

Sarai nodded. "I heard that many times in the women's quarters. I knew it from our histories."

"What did the priests of Elkenah do after they sacrificed Onitah's daughters?"

Sarai plaited the hair of the camel in front of her seat. "The people screamed for more blood. At a nod from the high priest, the lesser priests stormed down the stairs of the altar. They spread out, searching for someone. Abram. They took him and bound him to the altar." Sarai drew her fingers through the plaiting in the camel's hair, then plaited it again. "I joined Abram's prayers from where I stood near the edge of the temple enclosure. Even as far away as I was, I could hear his pleas to Jehovah."

"But Abram lives," I cried.

"Jehovah's angel appeared and clapped his hands, causing the altar and all the temple to crumble and loosen Abram's bindings. He ran from the altar, took my hand, and we ran from the temple complex. The priests died in the rubble."

I stared at Sarai with wide eyes. "Is that why you left Ur?"

Sarai nodded.

After that, Sarai and I spoke of belief in Jehovah and his commandments. It took time, but I slowly came to believe her faith came from an understanding of Jehovah.

I heard rumors the early Pharaohs believed in Jehovah and worshiped Him, as Sarai and Abram did, but they had no authority to sacrifice or complete other ordinances. Slowly, their understandings of Jehovah changed, and the people insisted on other gods to worship.

"Pharaoh prays to Jehovah still," Abram told me one day. "He told me about it on the day he insisted we leave his city."

I still respected Pharaoh, even though he had taken my friend Uat to bed. If he still trusted in Jehovah, I could.

One day after I agreed to become a worshipper of Jehovah, Abram and Sarai led me to a wide place in the river. I waded into the water with Abram. He lifted a hand and said a prayer, then buried me briefly under the water, baptizing me. This made it easier for me to live among these people.

We lived happily in Mamre for many years, with unhappy moments squeezing into the times. Less than a year after we settled there, I no longer washed the wadding Sarai used to protect her from her monthly bleeding. Her fertility had ended.

After that, I found her laying across her bed crying several times.

"Why do you cry?" I asked the first time.

"I wanted to give Abram a son. In all the time we have been married, I could not keep a baby within me long enough to give birth. Of all my desires, my desire to be a mother has been denied."

I put my arms around Sarai and held her close.

I have no man. Will I grow old without a child? Who would marry me when I belong to Sarai?

I wanted to sob along with her.

After this had happened three months in a row, I heard her arguing inside the tent with Abram. They rarely argued or lifted their voices with each other, and their argument caused turmoil within my gut.

"You must have a child," Sarai said. I could hear the pain in her voice. "You need an heir."

"No. I will name Danil's son as my heir. I will not set you aside for another," Abram's muffled voice said.

Oh, to be loved as Abram loved Sarai. I wanted that more than anything. But how?

Abram left the tent, his footsteps were just short of stomping away. He strode across our campsite with a straight back, staring forward. I could tell he was upset.

I decide to wait and not to go see if Sarai needed me. I heard her tears and sensed she needed to be alone.

Later, when I went in, Sarai still had wet eyes from crying, but she wiped them and feigned a smile. "We should begin weaving a blanket," she said.

A blanket? Why would she want to weave a blanket when she was so sad?

"Who is the blanket for?" I asked.

"I do not know yet, but I know we need to make one. Are you ready to learn how to weave?"

I nodded. I had wanted to learn that skill for some time.

One of Abram's men brought a loom in for me to use. Sarai had him set it next to hers inside her tent. Each morning after I completed the chores expected of me, I would sit beside her at my loom while she taught me to weave. My fingers did not like to move as they should, and I fought the weft threads that wanted to tangle into knots. My first blanket was not smooth, but it kept me warm.

After we finished the blanket, Abram moved my loom to my tent so I could weave when I had time. I no longer needed to wait for Sarai to be ready. Each of my next blankets became smoother and nicer to look at.

One day, a messenger came to tell Abram of the men gathering to battle against King Chedorlaomer. I learned he had formed an alliance with other kings and demanded tribute from all the kings of the lands in Canaan. Among the kings conquered by this King Chedorlaomer was the king of Sodom.

Lot and Galya had taken their flocks toward Sodom. I hoped they avoided the battles.

The kings grew tired of the demands and gathered their men to prepare for battle. Messages came warning Abram of the battle to come and reminding him that the large men called giants were among those who fought on both sides.

The messenger stomped away angrily. Abram had chosen not to join in the battle. The interloper king did not affect his lands. No tribute had been demanded from him, yet.

We heard stories of the battle raging near the Siddim or Salt Sea, detailing stories of horror as men died terrible deaths. Our herders kept the animals within the paddocks to protect them from wandering armies who would take what they wanted without thinking of us.

"Great armies require many animals to feed them," Abram said one evening at dinner. "However, I do not choose to make our animals available to them."

Some days, the battle echoed across the hills outside our home tents. I shuddered at the screams and the sound of clashing swords.

"Why does the battle not cross the hills into our valley?" I asked Abram one day.

"Jehovah protects us. As long as we trust Him, no army will attack us." He lifted his head.

When I could, I knelt in my tent and prayed to Jehovah for our safety.

We were protected for many days. Then, one day, the sounds of battle ended. I breathed more freely, knowing I did not need to fear the soldiers. The herders took the animals into the hills to feed on fresh, green grass once more.

Animals fed in the meadows again. Women spun the wool into thread and wove blankets and fabric. Children ran and played around the tents. Life returned to normal over time.

Until an injured man limped into the camp.

Sarai beckoned to me and I brought him a cup of wine. I joined the others in the circle of people who had gathered to listen to his story as he lay on a blanket in the shade of Abram's tent.

The man, Zed, shared a story that frightened me. "The battle raged for many days. It ebbed back and forth as some days the giants on our side fought off the other giants, pressing them back toward the sea. Other days, the giants who fought for King Chedorlaomer pushed us back against a cliff. We feared they would kill us all."

Zed took a sip of the wine in his hands, shaking so much I feared he would spill it. "It was a bloody time. Our arrows did not pierce the skin of the giants. We were forced to shoot them in the eyes to cause them any injury." The poor man clutched his arms to his chest.

"When they grabbed one of us," he said with a shudder, "they would shake us upside down or swing our bodies against the rocks. We had no chance against them."

It surprised me to see tears leak from his eyes. *Men don't cry, do they?*

"I ducked as one grabbed at me. Instead, he got my friend, Majid, who did not see the giant's hands coming his way." Zed gulped. "The giant grasped Majid by the head and swung him." He choked back a sob. "It was an ugly death."

Were not the giants human? How could they do such a thing to others? I could not imagine the hate one must feel to kill another in that way. My stomach churned as I listened to his story.

He spoke of fighting for days against them, giants fighting against giants and giants killing the smaller men in horrible ways. "They crowded us into a knot of men along the shore of the Siddim Sea. Our defense had collapsed. We raised our hands in defeat."

Zed bowed his head and sobbed. Abram allowed him to mourn for a time before pressing for more answers.

"What happened then?"

"They surrounded us and pushed us into a paddock as if we were cattle. Our kings could do nothing for us. I do not know where they were taken or where they went. Many hid among us, trying to blend in as mere soldiers. I suspect some ran to the mountains. Those not taken by our enemy."

Zed took another gulp of wine. "We waited in those animal paddocks for three days with little food or water."

"Then what?" Abram nudged Zed to continue.

Zed lifted his wine cup to his mouth and found it empty. He stretched it toward me as I was the one holding the jug. I filled his cup, and he slurped more, spilling some across his torn and bloody tunic.

I stretched out my hand to touch him, then pulled it back.

"People began to arrive from the cities, pushed forward in tight knots, and guarded by the giants. Camels and donkeys carried gold and silver from the treasuries and food and other goods from their stores of supplies."

Zed swallowed, then swallowed again. "My family was among the prisoners from Sodom. All but my aged mother and a young daughter who had succumbed to the vile treatment of their captors."

He eyed his cup of wine and drained it. "I will not share how they died. It is too horrible to remember." He stopped speaking, inhaling deep breaths. "It is better they went to live with the gods."

I shuddered. What horrible manner of death would cause a man to experience such pain?

"Lot? What of Lot?" Abram asked, leaning forward toward Zed. "Did he escape?"

Zed shook his head. "Lot and his family were taken as prisoners with all the others living in and around Sodom."

I bowed my head. How sad for Galya and her children. She had been good to me.

Zed gulped more wine and continued his story. "When all the cities were empty, they pulled out their whips and pushed us out of the coral and up the road toward Damascus. I do not know what King Chedorlaomer and the kings who supported him plan to do with their captives. Sell them. Use the women. I do not know." His gaze lifted to Abram's face. "I am sorry. I left Lot with those murderers."

"How did you escape?" Abram asked.

At last, he asked the question everyone wanted to know.

"Lot found me one day and told me to watch for a chance to escape. If I did, he implored me to come find you. He insisted you would come rescue him and avenge the loss of so many people."

Abram would rescue Lot and his family and avenge their losses? He did not have an army of men. How would he accomplish so great a task?

"And you found a way to escape?" Abram asked.

Zed nodded and straightened. "Late one night after they pushed us into a cave so they could drink a stash of wine they found, I walked along the edge of the cave, hoping not to be seen. Even the guards were drinking and were not as watchful as they should have been. They staggered along their guard line. Another man tried to slip past them ... and died for his efforts. I could not stay there and watch our people die and be sold as slaves. Lot's command to find you rang in my ears."

He breathed in deeply. "The guards had separated and the one giant closest to me staggered with his wine. He must have drunk barrels of it."

Abram brought his eyebrows close together. "And?"

"When he turned to march the other way, I slipped past him. I felt the rush of wind as his fingers brushed past me as I ran. I did not stop running until I knew no one followed me. The giant must have kept my escape to himself, rather than be disciplined by his leaders. I saw that discipline once. It was not pleasant to see, even if they were our enemies."

Abram rubbed his beard and nodded. "And you came here?"

"I did. I fell many times. They did not feed us enough to have strength to run or fight back. I ate whatever I could find — insects, plants, and an occasional mouse — to maintain the little strength I had."

Sarai waved to me. I moved closer to her. "He needs food," she whispered into my ear.

I bowed my head and returned to the cooking fire where a mutton stew for the evening meal bubbled. I dipped up a bowl of it, then carried it back to the circle of listeners and handed it to Zed with a spoon. He took the bowl and slurped it down, only pausing to chew on the mutton.

Rescue

Sarai and Abram stepped away from the group while Zed ate. From the determined look on his face, I knew he wanted to do something about it, something Sarai would not like.

It surprised me when she asked me to help her pack Abram's things.

"You will let him go rescue Lot?" I asked.

"I cannot stop him. He is a man," Sarai said with an impatient snort. "And, as he reminds me, Jehovah has promised him safety. He will protect Abram and his men."

Abram armed the young men he had trained to fight against wild animals with staves and swords. They organized into squads and fighting groups. He stayed up late with Zed, learning all he could about the kings and the giants. I heard their murmurings from my tent.

I wondered how Sarai could sleep while they talked. She probably did not. Knowing how she liked to be close to Abram, she would be sitting as near as she could, listening to their plans.

Early the next morning, I stayed with Sarai, Bara, and the other women, watching the young men follow Abram down the road toward Damascus. I wondered how many of these young men would return with Abram.

Eliezer, Bara's son and Abram's designated heir, stood tall beside his mother. Abram had given him the responsibility of caring for the people of Mamre and all the animals. Abram could not risk his heir and take him into battle.

The army marched down the trail and over the pass with swords glinting in the sun. As they disappeared, Eliezer called to the remaining herders and sent the animals off to the pasture.

With most of the men gone, the camp quieted until little boys found sticks and pretended to battle the giants and free the captured men.

They reminded me of the preening peacocks in Pharaoh's court. Silly little boys, like the boys of Egypt, playing at war. They would be men soon enough and follow a leader off to war. Why did men always believe they needed to battle?

The camp returned to its usual business as the animals grazed in the pastures and women spun and wove. Even so, there was an undercurrent of concern for the young men who traveled to fight with Abram. Sarai reminded us it would take time for Abram to catch up to the enemy horde before he could do anything to rescue Lot and his family.

I tried not to think of the many ways Zed had described giants killing the men and hoped none of our men would find death that way. I often joined Sarai in prayers for their safety.

After our men had been gone three weeks, men who had been captives began to straggle past our camp with stories of their release. It seemed impossible that Abram and three hundred eighteen men could have taken on the giants in those ways. I hoped Abram would share the stories with us when he returned.

Each time the men passed, women would ask about their men.

"None of your men were killed," the freed captives cried. "Their god carried them in his arms and protected them."

Each time Sarai heard these words, she dropped to her knees and offered a prayer of thanksgiving. I joined her.

In another three weeks, dust rose above the hills. Children rushed back from play on the hills shouting that our men had come home. Women ran to cook great pots of stew. Eliezer called for three cattle to be slaughtered. They soon hung over great cooking fires, waiting for the men.

Before long, our men marched over the top of the hill toward home, their swords still shining at their sides. Abram rode ahead on his white horse with the leaders of the fighting groups riding behind him.

Young men led donkeys loaded down with the wealth shared with them by the young leaders who received a portion of the riches taken from the kings. None of these were for Abram.

"I refused any spoils," he said. "My reward is the lives of our family and our men."

Sarai stayed close to Abram all that evening as we celebrated their return. I stayed close to my pot, dishing stew into the bowl of any who held it out. Although I rejoiced at their return, I had no one to celebrate, no one to cheer, no one to tell the story to me. Even as Sarai's handmaid, I was still an outsider.

Then a young man, Tomer, came and rested next to my fire. He had drunk too much wine and his story came out in pieces. He had been part of the second squad to enter the camp of the enemy. "We surprised the giants and their allies as we entered late in the night." Tomer shivered. "They had been drinking too much and did little to fight back. We slaughtered everyone, even the kings." Tears dripped into his beard.

I shuddered at the story and handed him another cup of wine.

Others passed by my cooking pot, sharing similar stories. They did not know whether to brag or cry about their battle.

"It was horrible," Tomer mumbled.

I took his hand and squeezed it. Tomer would be a nice man to share my life with, if Sarai and Abram allowed me to spend time with him. *I dream. Why would a man be interested in me?*

He leaned in to kiss me and fell against my chest. When he did not move, I pushed him away. He slumped to the ground, snoring.

Perhaps later.

Early the next morning, I heard the sheep and goats bleating, wanting to leave the paddock for food and water. I rose from my bed, expecting Abram to rush from his tent in search of food.

When he did not come, and none of the other men left their tents, the women came to me.

"Hagar, what should we do? Should we wake our men or should we take the animals out on our own?" Yael asked. "Our men drank too much wine last night. They will not wake, and the animals are hungry."

"We could take them," Bara said. "But I fear they will run away from us and make it more difficult for the men. The sheep do not know us like they know our men."

"I do not know what to do," I said. "I will go ask Sarai."

"She is still sleeping," Bara said with a gasp at my audacity.

"She will know what to do." I said.

I opened the tent flap and slipped into the darkness of Sarai's and Abram's tent. I had been in it often enough I could make my way through it without tripping. I listened beside the flap to their sleeping chamber before entering. Hearing no noise, I stepped in and walked softly to stand beside Sarai.

She slept peacefully. *She would. She had nothing to worry about. The most powerful man in the land loved her. What did she have to fear? Would I ever find this kind of peace?*

I brushed away my thoughts and touched her arm. Her eyes flew open.

"Mistress," I said in a low voice. "The women question if we should wake the men to take the animals to pasture."

"They celebrated late into the night. Let them sleep a little longer. The animals can wait."

"Yes, mistress," I whispered and crept from their tent.

The women waited outside. "The mistress says the animals can wait. Our men celebrated late last night."

"Much too late," Bara said, not trying to keep her voice low. "They know the animals need food and water."

"Listen to them bleat," Yael said. "They are hungry. What can we do while we wait for the men to wake? It could be well past midday if we allow them to sleep."

The women nodded and shuffled. "We should do something for the animals," one said.

Sarai stepped from her tent and joined us. "The sun is barely up. Should the men not have another hour of sleep to honor their victory?"

"Perhaps they should," Bara said, "but the animals should not be required to wait to eat. They were brought in early yesterday."

The sheep and goats continued their bleating.

"Can we take them to the pastures?" Sarai asked.

"Us?" a woman asked, her eyes bulging.

Sarai lifted a shoulder. "Why not? The animals are hungry."

"They do not know us as they know our men," Bara said, glancing around uneasily. "We discussed this earlier. What do we do if the sheep run from us? I have seen them do that when there is a new herder."

Sarai glanced at the circle of women and sighed. "Perhaps you are right. We should wake our men."

"Or our boys who go with the men each day," a woman said, leaning back as though she did not want to be recognized as the one speaking.

"The sheep would listen to the boys little better than they will listen to us," Sarai said. "It is time to wake our men. We should ensure they have a good meal to soften their lack of sleep."

"They did it to themselves," Bara smirked. "I am happy to have Danil home, but it is time he returned to his responsibilities."

"So be it," Sarai said. She turned toward her tent.

"You will wake the master?" I asked, following her hesitantly.

"I will. His sheep love him. They miss him as much as we did. Is there a meal ready for him?"

I nodded. "I have grains cooking, as always. I started them last night. And there is still some meat from last night."

"Thank you, Hagar," Sarai said, flashing me a smile. "I will go wake Abram."

She entered the tent and I returned to my cooking fire. I heard them giggling inside. Abram would arrive soon, needing food.

He strode through the tent door and sat at the low table, waiting for me to offer him food. I handed him a bowl of the cooked grains with some meat on top.

Abram gave me a smile and I returned it. He was good to me. I wanted a good man like Abram. Would I ever find one?

I turned away. Warmth from the fire flushed my skin.

Sarai joined Abram, and I offered her a bowl of grains and meat. She took it and began to eat, but her gaze never left me. Had I done something wrong? I tried to serve her as she desired.

After Abram left with the men to take the sheep to the pasture, Sarai returned to her tent without speaking to me.

I should not have wakened her. My stomach churned. What else could I have done wrong? I struggled to complete the tasks I normally did during the day as my mind whirled, trying to discover what I had done to cause Sarai problems.

When she came out later in the day, she acted as though she had no problems with me.

Confusion filled me. Earlier, she had glared at me like she would gladly chase me away. Now she treated me as though nothing had happened. Sarai did not usually behave that way.

After the evening meal, I walked through the camp, listening to the words of the women with their men. Loneliness filled my heart. I wanted a man to love, a man to care for me.

Tomer joined me, brushing his hands through his dark hair as I paced the edge of the camp. "You seem wistful."

"I am thinking."

He took my hand. "Are you angry with me? I did not intend to fall asleep on your breast last night."

I shook my head and laughed. "I was not offended and I am not angry. You had too much wine last night."

"We all did."

"All you men did."

He walked with me until we reached my tent. "Can I visit you again?" Timor asked.

He is not the best man here, but he is interested in me. Me. Not Abram or Sarai, but me. There is hope for me.

"I do not know your customs. Perhaps you should ask Abram or Sarai? Sarai is my mistress."

"I will. If they allow it, will you accept my visits?" He laid his hand on top of mine.

"If they allow it, I would be happy to accept your visits."

"Good," Timor said and leaned in to kiss me on the cheek before spinning on his heel and scurrying away.

I beamed after him, my hand against my cheek where he kissed me. One day, someone would kiss me on the lips. Perhaps it would be Timor.

Offer

Timor wandered past early the next morning. He waved and grinned at me while I bent over the fire to set the flat bread on the cooking rock.

I smiled back. My toes curled in my sandals.

He kept walking for Abram came out of the tent then. I did not blame him. Abram could be imposing, but I wanted him to stop and talk, just for a bit.

I had lived alone for too long, serving other women. I desired a man, my man. I saw others with their little children and wondered what it would be like to have a husband and a child.

I considered life with Timor. *He is young, but strong. He herds a flock of sheep. I heard those who herd get a portion of the lambs to grow their own flock. Timor would have enough to support us.*

I would not have to leave Sarai's service. I could not, since Pharaoh gave me to her. But I will not have to be alone all the time. I will no longer linger on the edges as the women speak of their husbands and children.

Jehovah, I am lonely. Would you bless me with a child and a husband? I desire to be a woman with a family like so many of these women.

Later that morning, as Sarai and I spun thread and I thought about how to ask her if she would allow me to consider marriage, she broke our silence.

"You may have heard Jehovah has promised Abram a great posterity."

My eyes widened. *How was that to be? Both were old, into their eighties, and they had no children. Worse, Sarai's womb had dried. She had told me of losing the child that had settled in her womb as a younger woman. I knew she could not have children at her age.*

"I did not know that," I said carefully as my scalp prickled a warning. "How do you think that will happen?"

"Jehovah will provide him with a child. Abram is not too old. I am."

I nodded. I had seen older men father children. Their seed did not grow too old to form children.

"We have been close for all these years. You have become a ... a sister to me."

After a quick glance at her, I shuffled my feet and continued to spin my wool. *After the way she treated me, how could she say we were like sisters? I would always be her handmaiden.*

"Sisters help each other. I have seen it in my many years."

I untangled a knot in the wool, then spun again before speaking. "I have seen sisters help each other, both here and in Egypt. I thought Uat was my friend. I did many things for her. And then she hurt me. Because of Uat, Senet sent me from her service."

"But you came to mine. That was good for me. Was it not good for you?"

I stared at my spinning. "It has been different for me. In some ways, it is harder, because we are so far from my mother and father. But it has been better for me to be far from Pharaoh." I grimaced. "I would not want him to take me to his bed or share mine."

"Pharaoh is an important man," Sarai said.

"And he gets what he wants."

"He did not get me." Sarai lifted her head.

"You were blessed by Jehovah."

"I would like you to be blessed by Jehovah," Sarai said in a slow voice.

"I would, as well. I am often lonely."

Sarai leaned closer to me. "Ah. I am sorry you have been alone for so long."

"I pray that my loneliness will end." I thought of Tomer and his gentle kiss the night before.

"I think I have a way to solve both our problems." Sarai bit her bottom lip.

I lifted my eyebrows. "Oh?"

"If you become Abram's concubine, you will no longer be lonely. You can bear him a child for us. You can be his concubine. I give you to him. Your child will be his and mine."

"His and yours?" My spindle slowed to a stop. I stopped breathing for a moment. Then I gulped a breath of air. "How would my child be your child?"

"He would be yours. I would be his auntie. Abram would have his son, and Jehovah's promise will be fulfilled."

And as your servant, my child would be yours.

"My son? A son with Abram? How is that any different from Pharaoh taking me?"

"Abram will not take you unless you and I both agree. I agree. I am offering you to him to be his concubine. He will be your husband, the father of your children."

"And I have a choice?" I asked.

"Yes, of course."

"Can I think about it?"

Sarai huffed quietly. She probably expected me to leap with joy to be offered her man to father my children. No joy here. I focused on my spinning as I waited for her to think.

"Yes. You must think about it."

"How long do I have?"

She bit her lips, then blew out her breath.

"I will pray about this, then let you know."

"That would be good."

I stopped my spindle and wrapped the wool. My muscles tightened and my heart raced. "May I go now? I need to walk and think and pray."

Sarai nodded. "You need to be sure you can do this."

Sure I can do this? I want to marry Tomer, not become Abram's concubine!

I swallowed. "Your request caught me by surprise. I will go think about this."

I hurried to my tent, set the spindle on my bed, and grabbed a shawl. I rushed out of the tent and walked away. I wanted to walk as far from Mamre as I could. Maybe even home to Egypt.

How could she ask that of me? Abram was old enough to be my father's grandfather. And Sarai wanted me to make a child with him.

I shuddered.

It would be almost as bad as lying with Pharaoh. Both men were powerful. Both were kings over their lands. I did not love either of them.

Did I love any man?

I could not say. I enjoyed the sweet kiss Tomer had set on my cheek the night before. That friendship could become love. If I did not accept Sarai's offer.

Was it an offer or a command?

She made it sound like an offer, a choice, but Pharaoh gave me to her. I was her slave. I really had no choice. Far from the river, out in this desert, the crocodiles had reappeared.

I wandered along the edges of the camp, staying away from the other women. Most of the men were either herding the animals or standing watch against any enemies. I could not see them, however, for my eyes filled with tears, spilling onto the front of my dress.

How could this happen to me?

As I walked along the outer edge of the camp, I prayed to Jehovah. Praying to him had become as natural to me as speaking to my mother had in the years I lived with her.

I poured out my frustrations and fear to Him, asking Him to help me know what to do. I enjoyed living here, far away from Pharaoh. I had become happy, except for my loneliness.

But I could not expect more kisses on the cheek from young men if I accepted Sarai's request.

Humph. I have little choice. She is my mistress. If I refuse and she sends me away, where will I go? My parents are far away, and they believed in other gods, not Jehovah.

I stopped as far away from Sarai as I could go and still be in the camp and perched on a rock.

"What shall I do?" I sobbed. "I am still young, able to find a husband and give him many children. If I accept this, I will have one child, give Abram his one child, and be left on my own. Will he care for us? I know Abram loves Sarai beyond the love my father had for my mother. How can I come between them?"

I sobbed until there were no more tears. I glared at the rocks at my feet.

A voice entered my mind.

"Hagar, my daughter," the quiet, manly voice spoke. "You are beloved for the faith you have had in me."

I jerked my head up and peered about me. No one was near.

"I have promised Abram a large family who will follow me," the voice continued.

My head bounced back up.

Again, no one could be seen.

"I will bless you with a son if you choose to accept Sarai's request. You and your son will be blessed. You will become a mother of a nation. If you are meek and submit yourself to your mistress, you will have a long and happy life and your son will be the father of a great nation."

"A great nation?" I murmured.

"A great nation of people. It will be your privilege to be the mother of multitudes. But you must choose."

I felt the voice withdraw from me, leaving me empty and questioning what I should do.

A son? A mother of multitudes? A happy life? If I submit myself to my mistress.

I exhaled. *How could I do this? Abram was an old man already. And Sarai expected me to love him? How?*

Memories of my interactions with Abram came into my thoughts. He had always been thoughtful and patient with me. I remembered his smiles, his gentle words, and his kindness.

Would he accept me as a concubine? Would he give me his time? Would I be less lonely?

I remained quiet and listened, waiting for the voice to return to my head. Although I did not hear it, a warmth filled me. I knew it would be right for me to accept. I shook my head. I did not want to make an old man part of the rest of my life. But it was right.

I bowed my head. "I thank you, Jehovah, for the answer to my prayers. I will accept Sarai's request. Please care for me."

I felt relieved at the thought. Now, I had to tell Sarai. She would have to work it out with Abram.

When I returned to my tent, Sarai perched near the cooking fire.

"I will do it," I said as I passed her. I did not dare stay to hear her reply but rushed into the sanctity of my tent.

I watched them at dinner that evening. Abram touched her hand and stayed close to Sarai. They shared soft jokes and quiet understandings. I could watch from the outside. Could we be a triad? Could I ever be a part of them?

I shuddered.

This would not be easy.

Concubine

"Men will move your tent," Sarai said to me the next morning. I jerked my head up. "Why?"

"Abram will visit you at night. I will not listen to the two of you together, doing what I could ..." she gulped, "... what I could not."

I hesitated. "Am I to continue to be your maidservant?"

Her eyes avoided mine. "You are. I have had a maid for so many years, I fear I would not know how to care for all my needs alone. And we have become friends, like sisters. I do not know if I could live without you."

"You would still want me?" I asked. My stomach tightened.

Her chin bounced. "I do. You have been a friend and a sister to me. When you have a child for Abram, we will become closer sisters. But I cannot listen to ... that."

I had not thought of that. I suspect I would struggle to listen to my husband and lover with another woman. I did not know. I would never have a husband who loved me as Abram loved Sarai.

Sarai opened her arms and I stepped into her embrace.

"I will not embarrass you," I whispered.

"I know."

"What happens now?" I asked.

"I must make an announcement in our Sabbath meeting to the others. I will give you to Abram. He will accept you, and you must accept him. Then you will be his concubine."

"And then?" I cleared my throat.

"He will join you in your tent for a time."

Until I carry a child within me. Then he will leave me.

"Will I be alone again, then?" I asked.

"No," Sarai cried. "You will be a part of our family. Always."

I believed her.

I did not say anything to anyone, but I no longer walked alone in the evening. I could not face having to tell Tomer that I could no longer accept his kisses, even on the cheek. He was a good man. I did not know if he deserved this any more than I did.

For the next week, Abram stayed with Sarai, holding her hand and caressing her. How could I ever expect the man to love me? He loved Sarai so deeply. If he took me, he would do it because she insisted, not because he wanted to do it.

I spent time alone in my tent, allowing the tears to fall where no one could see. I may have a man to give me a child, but I would not have a man who wanted me or loved me.

I dreaded the day when Sarai would share her decision with the community. She told me when she announced she had given me to Abram in a Sabbath meeting, it would be official, and he would take me as his concubine.

The following Sabbath, Sarai said nothing. Had she changed her mind?

The days passed between that Sabbath and the next. My emotions swung from joy to grief. Perhaps she would change her mind. I did not want to be given away to any man, especially one who did not want me. I had been given to Sarai and now to Abram. I had no say in this, even though she said I had a choice.

When the days were the darkest, the memory of the voice would come to my mind, comforting me. I would have a son. He would father a great nation. We would have happiness if I submitted to my mistress.

I wiped my eyes and walked from the darkness of the tent into the light. I could survive as the concubine of this great man if it really happened.

The next Sabbath, I sat beside Sarai as I always did while Abram led us in worship. I do not know what he said, for my mind whirled and my stomach lurched as I wondered if Sarai would announce her decision to give me to Abram.

Part of me hoped she had decided against her plan, but another part of me wanted her to do it. If she really wanted to do this, I wanted it done and over. The suspense and waiting hurt.

Before Abram could bring the meeting to a close, Sarai stood.

I sagged. She had determined to go on with it.

"I stand to announce something."

Abram stared at her, perhaps willing her to sit and not speak, but she continued. "I am old. You know I have no children. Abram deserves a child as an heir."

She turned her gaze to Eliezer, the man Abram had chosen as his heir. "You will receive an inheritance from us, but Abram needs a child from his body."

My heart sank. My stomach lurched. I bowed my head.

"For this reason, I give my handmaiden, Hagar, to Abram as his concubine."

A man gasped from behind us. Tomer. I wanted to go to him and explain. I could not.

She gestured for me to stand next to her. My stomach quivered. She took my hand in hers, then turned and took Abram's hand and set my hand in his.

"Any child of yours will be a child of ours. May you bring us posterity."

She stepped away and took her seat.

"Are you willing to accept me?" Abram asked. Sorrow filled his eyes, yet they held mine.

"I will." All the fear and concerns washed away.

Abram led me from the tent we used for Sabbath meetings. I heard the buzzing of people commenting, but he guided me to a tent, not the one I had used since coming to live in the desert, on the other side of the camp, far from prying eyes and ears, far from Sarai.

I slowly followed him, unsure of what would happen. Uat did not share her experiences with Pharaoh, but living with my parents, I had heard and seen much of their life as a couple at night.

But I had never kissed a man. Tomer gave me that sweet kiss on the cheek. I had never returned it. How was he feeling about this?

How did I feel? I had been given two weeks to prepare for this but did not know it would happen that day. I shook with fear.

Abram led me into the tent. He touched my arm.

"I know you did not expect this. Sarai can be determined. Do you think you can care for me a little?"

I mutely gawked at him.

"Even a little?"

"I may. You are my master. I was taken by Pharaoh's guards and given to Senet. Pharaoh gave me to Sarai, and now she has given me to you, retaining a portion of me for herself. Will I ever be my own person again?" My chin quivered as I tried to conceal the tears waiting to soak my dress.

Abram stepped close and lifted my chin. "Would you leave if you could?"

I rubbed the heaviness in my chest. "Where would I go? I cannot travel on my own. I doubt I could even return to my parents. They now have another child to take my place. What would I do?"

Abram encircled me with unexpectedly powerful arms. I had seen many men his age, but few with his strength. Perhaps his virility had not left him.

My whole body trembled in his arms. He ran his hand through my hair. "You have beautiful dark hair." He took out the pins that held it up, then brushed it back from my face. "A beautiful face, too."

I closed my eyes.

He kissed my eyelids. "I will be gentle."

We left the tent after dark, seeking food. Our encounter had left my chest tingling. We were surprised to find a pot of stew sitting on the edge of the fire, with two bowls and spoons waiting for us. Abram dipped stew into the bowls and handed one to me.

I cautiously tasted the stew. Had Sarai changed her mind about giving her husband to me?

But Abram showed no concern and ate with relish. I took another bite. It was good.

"Who cooked this?" I asked.

"Probably Sarai."

I lifted my eyebrows. "Sarai?"

"She learned to cook when we left Ur. The others did not want her to cook or work, but how could she not? She knew the others were busy."

"Sarai is a noble lady. Pharaoh wanted her. Why would she cook?"

"As I wanted her. She cooks because she chooses to cook. We all do what we choose to do." He closed his eyes and took a deep breath.

"Do we?" I asked.

"Hagar." Abram's voice rumbled with concern.

"I try to choose the right thing. I do not know if I chose this or if it was chosen for me." I slumped.

His powerful arms encircled me. "Perhaps it was chosen for you, but you accepted it. It is right."

I rolled my lips inward. "Yes. I did."

We ate our stew in silence, then returned to our little tent.

We stayed together, learning to care for each other as I learned to enjoy Abram's caring ways. He stayed with me for six nights.

"I must now return to my wife," Abram said on the sixth morning.

I stared at my feet, knowing in advance this would happen. He did not love me for me. He came to me and loved me because his wife demanded it of him.

"I will come to your bed sometimes," he said. "Return to your tent near us so you can assist Sarai when she needs it."

"I shall," I said.

He took me in his arms and kissed me. "I did not expect to care for you as I do. Thank you for your kindness to an old couple. I will be here for you when you need me," he whispered in my ear.

Then he left me alone.

More alone than I was before.

Now I knew what it was to be with a man, to have a man care for me, I liked it.

I wanted it.

I needed it.

But it was not for me. I could not have Abram all day and all night, every night. I had to share him with his wife and my mistress. And now, no other man would look at me or desire me to be his wife. I belonged to Abram and Sarai.

I allowed a sob to escape. I remained on the bed I had shared with Abram and wept into my hands a long time before I lifted my head and gathered the few possessions I had carried to my marriage tent.

When I had everything of mine packed into a basket, I wiped my eyes and took a long drink of water. I took time to brush my hair back, braid it, and dress in a clean dress. Then I picked up my basket and stepped out into the sunlight to return to my tent and my place in this world.

Would it be any different if Pharaoh had taken an interest in me? Would I slink home, hoping someone would care that it had happened?

I lifted my head, straightened my back, and stuck a smile on my face. No one needed to know my pain.

HAGAR, MOTHER OF SORROWS

I was Abram's concubine. He was mine, as he was Sarai's.

As I walked home, women called out to me, wishing me a happy day as I had seen them speak to Sarai. I spoke to them cheerfully. Some nodded to me in respect. Yes, my position in the world had changed.

By the time I reached my tent, the smile I wore had become real. I still would serve Sarai as she needed, but I was now more than her slave, her handmaid. I was not yet equal to her, I realized, but my position had changed.

I left my possessions inside my tent, picked up my spindle to spin while the food cooked, and walked to the fire to prepare the evening meal.

From inside the tent, I heard the noises of love, the same noises Abram and I had made the night before. I swallowed hard. This was to be part of my life now. I was to share my man with another.

Storm

Over the next weeks, Abram often crept into my bed, sharing his seed and his love with me. When I became unable to eat, he brought me fresh, juicy grapes and popped them into my mouth. The next morning, he brought me pomegranate and fed me the sweet, red, seeds.

"Do you carry my child?" he asked.

I gulped. "How do I know? I have never carried a child."

"When did you last have your womanly time?" He asked so sweetly I could not be embarrassed.

I thought back. "Before we came together."

"It is as I suspected. You carry our child."

Joy filled me. I would become a mother.

"You must not work so hard until the child settles in your womb. I fear that is why Sarai's child never settled."

I continued to prepare meals and spin. But Sarai had other women come to do some of the heavier chores for a month until she and Abram were certain I would not lose the child.

I became proud and walked with my head high, my shoulders thrown back. I had done something Sarai could not. I had a child within me. Abram loved me. He often came to spend the night with me.

Sometimes I allowed my pride to spill out. "Abram loves me more than he loves you," I softly whispered as Sarai and I worked together. Her head lifted and pain crossed her eyes, but she said nothing.

I grinned. Perhaps she believed it as well. It served her right. She forced me into this position.

I no longer lowered my head when I was with Sarai. I held it up proudly. I was not the mistress, but I had something she did not. I had a child growing in my womb.

"I am more of a woman than you," I murmured once.

Sarai did not even glance at me, but she grimaced.

We continued to work together, spinning and weaving. We began weaving blankets for the child. My thoughts sometimes slipped out of my mouth loud enough for Sarai to hear. "I am carrying the child you could never have."

She bit her lip and continued to weave.

I could not goad her into a response.

Why do I do this? She is an old woman. There is nothing she can do to make her life better or mine worse. Perhaps I do this to cause her the pain she caused me. I did not want her man. I wanted my own.

I heard her later that day, bitterly complaining to Abram. I nodded. She did feel.

The next morning, as we spun the wool together, my hateful words came out once more. "I carry the child you never could."

"And I gave you my husband for that child," she cried. "Abram is my husband. He loves me. He will always love me. If you do not stop your hateful whisperings, he will never lay with you again."

I tipped my head back and laughed. "He loves me more than you. He will soon spend all his nights in my bed, not yours."

An ugly, hateful look crossed Sarai's face. *At last she shows her feelings. Have I gone too far?* She swung her spindle at me, hitting me in the face.

I cried out.

She hit me again and again with her spindle. I covered my face and tried to avoid her. *How could an old woman beat me with such force?* Over and over, her spindle hit my hands and face.

Finally, I could take no more. I leapt to my feet and ran away from her, tears streaming down my face. I rushed past women who tried to comfort me. My feet carried me out of the camp and into the wilderness.

Even after my tears ended, I trudged into the wilderness. I walked and walked, not knowing or caring where I went.

Eventually, I slowed to a stop. The heat of the midday sun burned me and parched my mouth. I searched for water. I looked across the desert, searching for growing plants, anything that would show there was water. There was none.

I reached to my side for the water jug I often carried in my belt. It was empty. I had not filled it that morning.

My head pounded from the beating, my tears, and the sun. Now what would I do?

I turned back toward the camp. It had disappeared in the sand, although I saw the tracks of my feet in the sand. I could return.

But my pride would not allow it. I would not return to that hateful woman. I was better than her. I carried a child. She did not. I would be a mother to the nations Jehovah had promised Abram, not her.

I picked up a pebble and popped it into my mouth and turned away from camp. The pebble helped keep my mouth from sticking together, but did not give me much pleasure. No. I would not return now. Sarai would believe she had won a victory over me.

I walked toward a brush growing in the wilderness. I hoped it would have water of some kind keeping it alive.

I moved forward, stumbling to my knees too many times to count. I needed water. Where would I find it?

The gentle breeze that had kept me cool increased. With each step, it blew harder.

I wanted to live. But where?

I did not want to return to Sarai. She would beat me again for leaving her.

Hunger and thirst filled me. I wanted food, but I needed water. Surely there was a pool or a well out here somewhere.

I glared into the distance, planning to travel back to Egypt as I stumbled forward. I could do that. Abram may have his child, but he would not see it. I would defeat Sarai's plans.

I would travel south until I reached the trail wending toward Egypt. A caravan would find me and take me home to my parents. They would care for me and my child. They would be happy to have me home again.

I closed my eyes against the wind, wishing it would end. Instead, the gentle breeze became a raging windstorm. Wind blew bits of dust and rock, hitting me in the face and hands. I pulled my scarf across my face, but the fury of the wind dragged at it, fighting to tear it away.

I clung to my scarf, but the dust beat at my hands, burning. I feared it would shred the skin from them. I could not hide them within the folds of my dress, for I needed to hold my scarf.

The angry tempest raged, pulling at my clothing, whipping my hair from beneath the scarf and tangling it into knots.

I turned in a circle, hoping to see my footprints. The wind had blown them away. *Now what? I cannot find my way back, even if I want. Which way is south? What do I do?*

I tried to push through the storm toward the caravan road, but the wind blew me backward.

How would I find a caravan?

Sand filled the air. How would I find a caravan route, or even Abram's camp?

I pulled the scarf over my face and stumbled forward with a clenched stomach and a hurting heart. How could I find a home, any home, in this wind?

I collapsed to the ground. I could no longer move forward and did not know where to go, or even where I wanted to go. I dragged my scarf over my head and curled into a ball, praying the wind would slow.

I curled into a ball, trying to protect myself from the violence of the storm. I whimpered a prayer to Jehovah. I begged Him to protect my child. He had promised the child to Abram.

Some time later, I opened my eyes. I must have slept, for the wind had died. Still, dirt and sand filled the air.

My mouth felt as dry as the sand. I had not had anything to eat or drink since I had run from Sarai.

The dust slowly cleared. A fountain of water trickled near me. *I would have missed it if I had not stopped.* I crawled toward it, ready to drop into it and drink directly from it. However, a man offered me a cup filled with cool water. *Where did he come from? I do not care. He has water.*

I took it and gulped the water thirstily.

"You cannot drink so fast or you will be sick," the man said.

I slowed my drinking to a sip. He gave me three more cups of water before I waved it away.

"Who are you?" I asked. "Are you lost in this storm like I am?"

"I come to you as a messenger from Jehovah," he said.

Jehovah loves me enough to send me a messenger?

"Where did you come from? How did you come to be in the middle of the wilderness in a sandstorm?" the man asked. "And where will you go?"

"I fled from my mistress, Sarai, for she has treated me wrongfully," I said. I hoped he would agree with me. Sarai beat me. I had a right to leave her. Perhaps he would even direct me to a safe place to get out of the storm and find a home for me and the coming child.

Instead, he frowned.

I cringed from his terrible frown. This must be an angel from Jehovah.

"Return to your mistress and submit yourself to her."

"She beat me!" I cried.

"And you mistreated her."

I ducked my head. He was right. I had.

"You carry a son. You shall call him Ishmael, because the Lord has heard of your afflictions. He will be a wild and freedom loving man. He shall be among his brothers. Your children will multiply to numbers beyond counting, as the sands in the desert."

I bowed my head.

The wind returned. I opened my eyes. The angel had left me alone in the storm.

I remained beside the fountain, considering the messenger's words. I had been haughty, my behavior unkind and thoughtless.

I had to return to Abram and Sarai.

I turned toward where I thought the camp was and tried to walk that direction. The wind blew against me, beating me back, tearing at my clothing, scraping my skin.

I bent into the wind, fighting against it.

I would take one step forward and the wind blew me back as far as I had traveled. It knocked me to the ground. I stood up and struggled forward each time it blew me over.

At last, I crawled a distance. Once I slept in the middle of the raging storm. Jehovah would get me back to Abram and Sarai or he would not have told me to submit to her.

When I woke, I pushed onward once more. The wind harried me from all directions. I was determined to do as commanded by the angel. I had to return.

Day returned, but it brought only a hazy light.

I continued to fight against the wind, bent to protect the little one within me, driven to find the camp and Sarai. I needed to make amends for my actions. I would give Abram his child. I would bear Ishmael. I would have a son.

I said these words over and over, step after step, fighting the wind.

Then, strong arms lifted me.

"Hagar, I found you."

Abram! He came for me!

"I will give you a son. His name will be Ishmael," I mumbled.

"You will be safe. I will carry you home."

He gave me a sip of water and a bit of a date, wrapped me in a blanket, and lifted me into his arms. Then he turned into the wind and marched toward home. He stopped occasionally to give me water and to check the blanket that surrounded me. I was safe in Abram's powerful arms. He would get us home. Along the way, I could no longer stay awake.

I awoke to someone brushing my hair. "That feels wonderful," I mumbled.

"You are awake!"

Sarai. She would brush the sand from my hair after all I had said to her?

"I have worried for you since you ran from me."

I moaned and gawked around me. I was in my tent, on my bed. I inhaled a deep breath and groaned at the pain in my chest. "I was wrong to taunt you."

The brush did not stop moving in my hair.

"Jehovah sent an angel to me in the midst of the storm." I looked up into Sarai's eyes. Her chin quivered. "He told me to return to you and submit myself to you."

Tears dripped onto me from Sarai.

"Are you injured?" she asked. She swept the brush through my hair once more, then set it aside.

"Bruised from falling and sore from the wind's attempts to tear my skin off my body. But, no. I am not injured."

She set her hand on my arm. "When you are ready, I will bring you hot water for a bath."

I struggled to sit with a sigh. "You are my mistress. I should bring you bath water."

"Tomorrow, perhaps. Allow me to bring you water. I beg you to forgive my cruelty. I should never have hit you."

Would I forgive her? Could she forgive me?

I finally pulled myself up to sit in the bed. "And I should not have taunted you and caused you such pain. I forgive you if you will forgive me."

She stared into my eyes. "You are forgiven."

The tent door opened and Abram peeked in. "Are you covered?"

I nodded, and he pushed the flap of the door all the way open and stepped back. A man carried in a tub. Others followed with steaming buckets of hot water. When they poured in their bucket of water, they backed out of the tent, entering again and again until the tub filled.

"You can have a bath and clean the sand from your skin," Abram said. "When you are clean and able, please come talk with us."

I nodded once more. Abram motioned for Sarai to follow him.

"Can you do this alone?" she asked.

I squeezed my eyes shut. "I am able, thank you. Go with Abram."

When my tent door fell closed, I shakily stripped off my sandy clothing and stepped into the tub. The hot water felt delicious. I lay back in it for a long time, soaking away the pain of the windblown sand.

At last, I took up the soap and a cloth and carefully washed my body, noticing the scratches from the driven sand. Perhaps I had more injuries than I knew.

The babe within me fluttered.

I grinned.

"Ishmael. You have a powerful father. He may be old, but he is strong."

I submerged beneath the water to wet my hair, then scrubbed away the last of the dirt. Thankfully, Sarai had brushed most of it away.

When I was clean once more, I stood and let the water drip from my body. A small bump extended from my belly. It had begun to swell. It would not be long before all within the camp knew I carried Abram's child.

I touched the growing place. "Stay put, Ishmael. The angel said you would be strong."

I dried and dressed, leaving my damp hair flowing loose across my shoulders. Abram and Sarai waited. I could braid it later.

Abram and Sarai waited for me in their tent. I closed my eyes and offered silent thanks to Jehovah.

I scratched at their tent door.

"Come," Abram called.

I entered. He sat with his chair, touching Sarai's chair, and holding her hand. They were still together, even after what I had done and Sarai's response. I closed my eyes briefly, then knelt in front of them.

"I come to beg your forgiveness for all the trouble I have caused. I thank you, Abram, for coming to my rescue. I do not know if I could have returned to your tent in the storm without your help."

Abram took my hand. "I forgive you. You are part of our family. I could not allow you to struggle alone in the wilderness."

Yet you waited until after the storm nearly blew me away. You have your reasons. I forgive you.

I turned to Sarai. "I grieve for the heartache I have caused you. Please forgive me for the harsh and prideful words I spoke."

She lifted me from my knees. "I told you many years ago I would stand by your side as long as you are faithful to me."

Stand by me while I carry your child. "I will work to be more faithful," I whispered.

"That is all I ask," she said.

I stepped into her arms and held her tight. "I will never forget again. I will remain faithful to you."

I told them all that had happened in the wilderness. Abram questioned me about the words the messenger had given. He had promised me much of what Jehovah had promised Abram.

Abram pulled me into an embrace. "We feared for you, for your safety, while you were gone."

"You feared for your child," I whispered.

"Yes, Hagar. I feared for Ishmael, although at that time I did not know his name. More importantly, Hagar, I feared for his mother. We are grateful you found your way home."

"I was led here, with your help," I said.

"And we are glad you were," Sarai muttered.

Ishmael

Over the next several months, I worked with Sarai as I had before, cooking and cleaning, and doing the chores while my baby grew within me. Slowly, my body expanded, making it difficult to reach things. Even worse, I could no longer bend over to pick things from the ground. During this time, we worked together to prepare for Ishmael's birth. We spun yarn and wove blankets and soft fabrics from which we stitched tiny clothing.

Neither of us had any experience with babies, but Bara and others in our community did, and they were happy to help.

About eight months after Sarai gave me to Abram, the other women celebrated the coming birth with me. They brought gifts of little things I had not thought to prepare.

"We knew you would not know to have this," Adi, Shemaya's wife, said. She was a young mother with three little children. "I did not think about these things."

"There were many things I did not consider," Yael said. Her children were nearly grown. "Even though the other women spoke of them, I did not think I would need such things. I learned quickly that I did."

The women laughed together. They formed a society of mothers that I would soon enter. They wrapped me in their love like the warm blanket Abram had carried me home from the wilderness in.

Ishmael enjoyed the attention as well. His foot kicked my belly in time to the laughter. I rubbed at the spot.

"He is active?" Yael asked.

I nodded. Just then, Ishmael kicked me hard enough that all could see my stomach rise and fall.

"He is a strong one," Sarai said.

"He will be a leader," Bara said, touching the spot.

I ducked my head and smiled. I knew what the messenger had said about him. Wild and free. Would that make him a good son for Abram?

I did not care. He was my son. He could be wild. I was happy to have a child.

Five weeks later, I was not as certain of that choice. A clenching pain in my stomach began slowly. Tiny pains clutched and let go. Then my water broke during the night. I remembered what Bara had told me. If waters fled from my body, it would be time for Ishmael's birth.

I dragged the wet bedding from my bed and looked for the pile of old bedding Bara had instructed me to have ready. Before I could pull it across my bed, I doubled over with a strong, seizing pain.

I bent over and grabbed at my belly until the pain disappeared. Sighing in relief, I grabbed the old bedding and tossed it across my bed. It did not lie flat and beautiful, but they served their purpose.

Another pain gripped me. I fell down on the bed and fought through the pain.

Eventually, the sun had risen. I should have been preparing the morning meal for Abram and Sarai, but I could not leave my bed. The pains were strong, with little time to rest between them. I rolled back and forth in the bed, seeking a position that would alleviate the pain.

The door to my tent opened. "Hagar!" Sarai cried. "What is happening?"

"Cramps. Stomach." I could not speak complete sentences through the pain.

"Is it time for the child to come?" She caught my hand and squeezed. Someone cared enough to help take the pain.

"How do I know?" I wailed.

"I will go get Bara. She will know. She has brought many children into the world." She lifted her fingers out of my clutch. "I will be back soon."

I grabbed for her hand, not wanting her to leave me alone with this pain.

"I will return."

She ran from my tent. My hands sought the pain in my belly, hoping the touch would ease it as it had so many times before.

My stomach was hard like a stone. As I held my hands on it, it relaxed and the pain eased. I panted as I rested until my stomach hardened again, bringing with it increased pain.

I yelped and cried. As it eased, my stomach softened. They were connected some way. Why had no one told me about this?

Not long after, I felt my stomach tighten again. I sucked in a breath and held it, hoping to hold in my cries, but it did not help. I expelled my breath in a long scream.

Sarai rushed back into my tent. "Bara is coming. She is gathering her supplies."

I grabbed her hand. "Stay with me. Mothers in Egypt died in childbirth."

"You will not die," Sarai said. "Bara will come soon to help you." She brushed my damp hair from my forehead.

"You think I will not die?" I moaned.

"No. The angel promised you a healthy son. You will live to help him grow. I have heard that giving birth is difficult, but you can do it."

I gripped her hand as the next wave of pain brought a hardened stomach approached.

"Stay with me, Sarai," I begged. I wanted her with me. Was it because she was the closest thing I had to a mother, or because I wanted her to see the pain she and Abram had caused me? I do not know. I doubt I will ever know.

I gave myself to the pain, gritting my teeth and clenching my fists as it increased, unaware of hurting Sarai's hands. I only learned later that I squeezed them tightly enough to cause her pain.

Bara bustled in and said something I could not hear as I concentrated on my pain. As it eased, Sarai eased her hand from mine. "Hagar, I need to go take the grains from the fire."

I did not want to be alone with this pain. "Come back."

The pain returned, demanding I pay attention to it. I screamed. The pain subsided and I lay panting in my bed.

Bara moved from one side to the other. "Good girl. You changed your bedding already."

"I drenched the others."

"Ah. A good sign the babe will come soon. How long has this been going on?"

"Since before dawn. It was not yet light when I changed my bedding."

Bara stepped to the door and scanned the sky. She hummed to herself. I briefly wondered what it meant, but my stomach hardened once more and the pain came with it. I screamed Sarai's name. Why did she do this to me?

Sarai appeared at my side once more. "I am here."

"Why did you not tell me it hurts this much?" I demanded through my panting.

Her voice filled with sorrow. "I did not know. I have never experienced birthing a child. Did you not ask Bara and the other mothers?"

The pain had caused me to tremble all over. "I spoke to them, but somehow I did not understand."

"How could you? I am here to help. Grip my hand." She set her hand in mine and I held it tight as the hardness returned, bringing searing pain with it.

I screamed through the pain.

Bara touched my feet. "You are doing well. Scream if you need. It helps push the child from your body."

I squeezed my eyes shut and tried to control the trembling.

"You are doing well," Sarai repeated. "Bara says it will not be long."

"Not if the pains come as hard as the last one. Here comes another. It will not be long," Bara agreed.

How could she tell? Could she see my stomach clench as it hardened? I no longer cared.

The pains seemed to never end, one rolling on top of another. I screamed until I could scream no more.

Bara invaded me with her fingers. By then, I did not care. If it would bring Ishmael from within me, she could do what she wanted. "He will come with the next pain. Do not push yet, let me turn his head."

How was I to do that? But I held my breath during the next spasm. She did something within me.

"Push down when the next pain comes," she ordered. "It will push your son out of you."

The pain came immediately and I pushed and pushed.

"He is almost here," Bara called as the pain dropped from me. "Do that a few more times and your son will be born."

This would end? How could I make it end faster? The pain built, and I pushed my stomach muscles, straining to push the hardness out from between my legs.

"Once more should do it," Bara called from near my feet.

She said that earlier. I gulped air into my lungs.

My stomach tightened and I pushed and screamed as hard as I could. Suddenly, I felt the hardness slip through.

I lay gasping for breath. It was over.

"One more push, dear," Sarai said. "Ishmael needs the rest of his body to come out."

"Can Bara not pull him out?" I whimpered.

"No," Bara said. "You must push it out. You are nearly finished."

My stomach tightened again and I pushed.

"You have the son you were promised," Bara called.

I lay back against my pillow as Sarai brushed my hair back away from my face. I would not do this again. Too much suffering.

"Ishmael is here," she crooned.

I could only glance her way.

I heard a slap and the angry cry of a child.

Bara set the child on my belly. "We need to separate him from you," she said. "Keep him from falling."

I set my hands on either side of him and waited, then she lifted the child from my body. I missed him already.

"I must clean him for you, then we must remove the afterbirth."

Good. I was finished with the pains.

Bara lay a bundle in my arms. "Meet your son. Hold him. You will have another pain."

Fear filled me. Not another.

"It will not be as bad. You must expel the afterbirth." Bara massaged my stomach until another pain hardened it.

"Push once more," she called.

I pushed until I felt something come from within me.

"It is finished," Bara said. "You can rest."

Bara and Sarai helped clean me up and helped me suckle Ishmael, who had cried since Bara cleaned the birthing mucus and blood from his body. Sarai left the tent and returned with Abram.

Bara gathered something into a rag and walked out of my tent, holding the tent flap open for Abram. "You have a beautiful son," she said.

I felt eyes on me and looked up. Abram gazed at me and our son, his eyes filled with love.

He came and knelt next to me. "He is beautiful," he whispered.

"He is," I answered. "Would you like to hold him?"

"May I?" Abram rose and leaned over us.

"Sit," Sarai said, pointing to a stool near my bed. "I will put him in your arms."

Sarai had claimed the babe and me as hers. At the time, I did not care. I was happy to have Ishmael born and in our arms. He was my son, mine and Abram's. We shared something she could only dream of.

Sarai lifted the little boy and snuggled him close to her chest before handing him to his father.

"He is red and hairy," Abram said.

"All babies are red and hairy," Bara said as she entered the tent. "That will change. I am here to finish cleaning Hagar."

She washed my legs and belly, then pulled a clean blanket over me. She patted my leg. "You did a good job. I will leave you alone to be a family."

I glowed in her praise. I did something I never thought I could do, something Sarai had never done.

"Family," I whispered. "I did not think that word would ever include me again."

Abram settled Ishmael in one arm and reached to smooth my hair from my face. "You are part of our family. You and Ishmael."

I did not know how to feel about that. I was happy to be part of a family. However, I wanted that family to consist of only my husband, our children, and myself. I had not expected to be part of Abram and Sarai's family.

Abram leaned over and kissed me on the forehead. Ishmael opened his eyes and squalled.

"I hear he may need a dry bottom cloth," I said. I felt his bottom cloth. Drenched.

I directed Sarai to bring me a clean cloth. Abram laid the child on the bed beside me and together we worked to change his wet cloth.

When we had it changed and the blanket enfolding Ishmael once more, I lifted him to my breast to help him stop crying.

"He lets us know what he needs," Abram said.

"The messenger said he would be strong," I murmured.

"It looks like he will be that," Sarai agreed.

Abram and Sarai stayed with me through the rest of the day, helping me to care for Ishmael. I slept while they watched him sleep in his little basket bed.

I woke with Abram lying next to me, his arm surrounding me. I peered toward the baby's little bed. "Is Ishmael well?" I asked.

"He sleeps. Sarai went to get us food. You must be starving."

My stomach rumbled. I set my hand on it. It felt strange with the bulge gone.

I giggled. "I am hungry."

"That is good," Sarai said, entering the tent. "I brought us food."

She carried a pot of stew and a basket with bowls, spoons, and flat bread.

"This will help you heal faster," she said. "Bara told me a thick soup or a stew would help replace the blood you lost."

I inhaled the delicious smell. "It smells wonderful! I have not eaten since last night."

Sarai dished up stew into bowls and brought the first to me. I hungrily dipped my spoon into it and started eating.

"We should offer Jehovah thanks," Abram reminded me.

We did. I needed to thank Jehovah for my healthy child. I set my spoon down and attempted to get out of bed.

"You do not need to kneel. Not tonight. You can pray from your bed with us," Abram said.

He and Sarai knelt on the floor and lifted their arms. Abram thanked Jehovah for the safe delivery of Ishmael into this life and for my safety. I bowed my head in agreement. "Thank you, Jehovah, for Ishmael," I added in my head.

That night, Abram slept next to me, holding me in his arms. Sarai slept on a pallet of blankets on the floor beside the bed. When Ishmael woke, she would change his cloth and bring him to me so I could rest.

Each day for a week, the three of us stayed together in my little tent. Abram and Sarai watched over me and my child while I slept and healed from the birth. We were a family. After so long alone, I enjoyed it.

Much as I appreciated their help, I breathed a soft sigh when Bara determined I was well enough to be alone with my child once more. I needed to rest another week, but I did not require Sarai and Abram to spend every minute with me.

Sarai continued to bring me meals each day. Abram came often to hold our child and spend time with me. He slept with Sarai every other night, and me on the other nights.

After two weeks, I left my tent carrying Ishmael in his basket bed. I nudged Sarai aside and prepared the morning bread to eat with our grains.

She smiled at me and sat in her chair. "Are you up to this?"

"I am. I am ready to do more than sit in bed and care for my babe."

I mixed the bread and patted it in thin circles before setting it on the rocks in the fire.

Abram came out of Sarai's tent. "Oh ho," he cried. "You are well enough to cook again?"

"I am." I spooned grains into a bowl and gave it to him.

He took my hand and squeezed it. I smiled into his eyes. He did love me.

After we ate and I took care of Ishmael, Abram left to tend to the sheep herders while Sarai and I cleaned up. We then went into her tent and worked together to weave fabric.

I watched with pride as Ishmael grew. He grew fast, doing those things children do, lifting his head, turning over, cutting teeth, crawling, and eventually walking.

He followed his abba as soon as he could walk. I often saw him riding above the men on Abram's shoulders. It made me smile. Sometimes Sarai would join me at the edge of our living space, watching Abram with Ishmael.

Before he could toddle, Abram gave him a kitten Ishmael called Ca. He loved that cat. It would let him carry it. When Ca got big, his feet often dragged along the dirt, but he still allowed Ishmael to drag it in his arms.

He loved the animals. As he grew older, he shared his love with the dogs, sheep, and goats. Any animal he could see. We had to watch that he did not try to pet the wild animals.

He was a cheerful boy who soon tried to do many things on his own. When he learned to speak, he called Abram Abba while Sarai was Aunty. Sarai seemed to love and admire him as much as I did.

Ishmael's strength grew along with his frame.

"Is that Ishmael going with the herders?" Sarai asked one morning.

I glanced up from washing our clothes to see my little boy of only four racing behind the herders as they took the sheep to feed in the hills.

"Ishmael!" I called. "Ishmael."

He turned. "Yes?"

"You are not big enough to go with the herders. Come home."

Benayah turned and called, "I will ensure he returns safely."

My little boy was too young to go into the hills with the herders. "He will get in your way."

Benayah shook his head and laughed. "No. Ishmael will help us. He will be no problem."

"If you are certain?"

"I am." The man and my son turned and marched up the hill, wending their way to the front of the sheep.

Sarai shook her head and laughed. "He leads everyone like his toy."

I laughed with her and agreed, then returned to our washing.

Ishmael's confidence grew as he helped the men. He led the other boys as he did the sheep after returning from the hills with the herders. He ordered them about, and they did his bidding.

"Why did you make little Joel cry today?" I asked one evening when Ishmael was eight.

"He is a crybaby. He wanted to join the big boys, but his legs are not big enough to keep up. He was crying for us to slow down."

Ishmael had joined the men long before his legs were long enough. They had slowed for him. "So, why did you not slow down?"

"He needs to get stronger."

"Perhaps, but when you were littler, the older men were kind and waited for you."

"Because I am Abram's son. They did not wait for other boys."

"Because you are Abram's son, you should wait for the littler ones. You are their leader. You should be an example."

He laughed harshly. "Joel can keep up or wait until he is strong enough to run with us."

I lifted my eyebrows. "Is that what your father would do?"

Ishmael hung his head. "Probably not." He lifted his head and peered at the boys waiting for him to return to him. "But Joel is little."

"His legs are shorter than yours. Give him a chance to grow."

"Mother," he whined, with his fists on his hips.

"Ishmael," I retorted, copying his stance.

"Yes, Mother. I will slow down for Joel." He raced away to his friends. They started to speed away from Joel, then Ishmael slowed. "Hurry, Joel. We will wait for you."

His consideration for Joel lasted only the one day. After that, Ishmael expected Joel to keep up with them.

Abram spoke to him about it, but he shrugged.

"He will have to learn to run faster to keep up," Ishmael said with a grin.

Abram shook his head. The boy was a wild one.

It was difficult to chasten him, for he would grin in a way that made me laugh with him. He made me proud as he went each day with the herders, no longer needing Benayah to supervise him. Ishmael had made himself a part of the team long ago.

He gave his gang of friends orders and expected them to follow them, seldom backing down when they argued against it.

I was concerned that he had a hard edge. He never gave in when Joel cried for him to slow down. Eventually, Joel grew and ran as fast as the rest of them.

Life was good for us. Ishmael and I were part of Abram's family. The others in camp looked up to us. The women asked me for direction as much as they asked Sarai. I had become important.

Covenant

Then, one day, Abram spoke with Jehovah.

He shared the news with Sarai first, then called Ishmael and me in to tell us the news, taking Sarai's hand in his.

"Does that happen often?" Ishmael asked, tilting his head to the side.

"No. He does not often speak to me. However, He has spoken to me before a few times." He took a deep breath and let it out slowly.

"What did He say to you this time?" I asked. I remembered his other visits with Jehovah. They were always much more intimidating than my visit with the angel before Ishmael's birth.

He lay his hand across his breastbone. "I have obeyed His commandments, and He changed my name to reveal it. I am no longer Abram. I am now Abraham, Father of Nations."

I gasped. "Can Jehovah do that?"

Sarai nodded. "He can."

"Ab-ra-ham." I tried the new name out. "It is much like the name your father gave you."

"It is," Abraham said. He looked into Sarai's eyes and squeezed her hand. "And He changed Sarai's name as well."

Ishmael looked at her. "What did Jehovah change your name to? Saraith?"

She tittered. "No. I am now Sarah."

"Why would Jehovah change your names?" I asked. "Did he change mine?" I held my breath.

"No. You are still Hagar," Abraham said.

158

I released my breath, uncertain if it made me happy or sad. "Good. I did not want to lose the name my father gave me. I have already lost so much."

"That is true," Abraham said.

"Why the name change?" Ishmael asked.

"I have made another covenant with Jehovah," Abraham said. He swallowed and glanced at Sarah. "You know Jehovah promised I would be the father of a great nation."

"And you will be, with Ishmael," I said.

"Yes, Ishmael will father a great nation. But Sarah will also give me a son who will also father many children."

I turned my gaze toward Sarah. She was seated beside Abraham, her skin wrinkled and dry, like her womb.

I laughed. Not possible.

"I laughed as well," Sarah said. "How can an old body, dried and worn like mine, conceive a child? It is impossible."

Abraham squeezed her hand again. "Remember, nothing is impossible with Jehovah."

"It is hard to believe," Sarah said.

I nodded.

How could she conceive a child? Jehovah would have to do lots of work for that to happen.

Abraham turned to me. "You need not fear. I will always care for you and Ishmael. He is my first-born son. But Sarah's son will receive the inheritance."

My blood boiled. "Her son? When she gave me to you and Ishmael is first?" I almost shrieked.

Ishmael crossed his arms and bounced his feet..

"It is the law of Jehovah. Children of the first wife are first. Children of the concubine come last."

I bit my lip. Last? After all they put me through? I could have had a husband and been his first wife if Sarai had not given me to Abram!

I blew out a loud breath. "That is not fair."

"Fair or not, it is the law."

I closed my eyes and shook my head. *It does not matter. Sarai, or Sarah, cannot have a child at her age. Ishmael will be the only heir.*

"Part of this covenant," Abraham continued, "is that all men in our community, men and boys, bond and free, are to be circumcised."

Ishmael had been fiddling with his robe, but now jerked his head up. "All men and boys? What is this circumcision?"

"Our foreskins will be removed."

My eyes opened wide. Not my Ishmael.

"It is a token of the covenant made with Jehovah. If a man or boy cannot accept this token, he can no longer live here with us. Can you do this, Ishmael?"

"Will it hurt?" Ishmael asked, staring between his feet.

"Probably." Abraham's lips pursed.

Ishmael bit his lip. "Do this or leave?" His eyes lifted to meet Abraham's eyes.

Abraham nodded.

After a brief pause, Ishmael looked up. "I will do it."

I inhaled sharply.

"Good. We will call a meeting of the camp. Run to all the home tents. Tell everyone to join us in the open space in front of our tent."

Ishmael nodded. He jumped up and ran from the tent.

"I will talk with the women and prepare them for what is coming," Sarah said.

As she left, I regarded at Abraham. "Are you certain of this?" I asked.

Abraham held my eyes with his gaze. "I am certain. Jehovah has commanded it."

"All of this?"

He nodded. "All of it."

I pinched my lips together, refusing to say anything, and left to join the group of women. My child would require Dara's healing help. When she shared the salves, I would need to care for Ishmael. I left the women's meeting and stood silently near the edge of the men. I worried about the pain Ishmael would endure. Later, I learned that we women would protect our camp while our men healed.

Abram, I mean Abraham, told the men about the covenant he made with Jehovah and the new requirement. A roar rose from the men as they discussed the requirement.

"I will go first," Ishmael said.

"If the lad will do it, I will," Eliezer said, stepping forward to be next. The other men and boys came forward, all willing to make the covenant with Jehovah.

Abraham stepped in front of Ishmael. "*I* will go first. Danil, you do it for me, then I will do it for all the others."

"Then me, Father," Ishmael said.

"Yes, then you, Ishmael."

I crept away to my tent to prepare the bandages and ointments for my son.

When Ishmael returned to our tent, bent over from the pain, I tended to his injury. The other men and boys went back to their tents to be tended by their wives and mothers. It took about a week for the men to walk normally again. We were blessed during the time the men healed, for no enemy attacked our encampment.

Our men had done their part in the covenant Jehovah made with Abraham. Now, we would see if Sarah would conceive a child, a boy child.

I had not had enough experience with Jehovah yet to trust He would open her womb. In truth, a part of me hoped He would not..

161

One evening, about two weeks after our men had healed, I worked near the fire, preparing our evening meal, when three strangers walked along the path toward our tents. Abraham leapt from his seat in front of his tent and called to Sarah to make three fine cakes for them.

Better Sarah than me. I was tired that day. *We worked hard. These must be important visitors for Abraham to ask Sarah to make fine cakes for them rather than me.*

Abraham called to Joel to prepare a young calf and roast it to feed the visitors.

I lifted my eyebrows. Important visitors indeed.

As I was not needed, I continued to watch Abraham and our visitors, who relaxed in the shade of the cedar tree, from the entrance to my tent. Before long, Sarah brought out the cakes, and Joel brought the meat. Sarah returned to her tent. I could see her shadow near the entrance, where she listened.

The men sat together, eating and visiting. When they had eaten everything, one visitor asked, "Where is your wife, Sarah?"

I expected her to hurry out to see to the visitor's needs, but she did not.

Instead, Abraham answered for her. "My wife, Sarah, is inside the tent, resting after a long day."

The visitors soon rose to leave. One said, "I will return in the time it takes for a life to grow in a womb. In that time, your wife, Sarah, will have a son."

I gulped and fought back a laugh in time to hear the visitor lift his voice enough for Sarah to hear.

"Why does Sarah laugh and say she is old? Is anything too difficult for Jehovah? Trust Him. All things are possible in Him. When I return, Sarah will have a baby son in her arms."

I had heard Sarah laugh too. She must not have believed all that Jehovah had promised.

Sarah stepped from the tent. "I did not laugh. I know all things are possible."

My desire to laugh ended. I do not. I doubt you will have a son.

"No. You laughed," the visitor said. "See what Jehovah can do. He can heal a dry womb like yours."

The visitors left. Abraham accompanied them to the road before returning to his tent. I watched them leave, thinking I must ensure the evening meal did not burn. I wanted to listen in, to hear what Sarah would say about the visitor's message, but I did not. Instead, I stirred the soup and prepared bread.

Abraham and Sarah were late coming to eat the evening meal that day. By the time they came out of the tent, Ishmael and I had eaten our bowls of soup and bread. I hurried to fill Abraham's bowl before I served Sarah, as I always did.

I waited for them to share with me the message of the visitors, but they kept it to themselves.

I heard the message, but it was not mine to share, so I anxiously waited to see what would happen.

Abraham and Sarah spent more time alone in their tent than usual. He did not come to me as he usually did.

For the next three days, I watched Abraham climb the hill near our camp. I wondered what his concern was. When he returned, his hair hung limply to his shoulders. Strands of white streaked through his dark hair.

I wanted to hear what had happened. Abraham called Ishmael and me in later to tell us the story.

"As I peered toward Sodom and Gomorrah where Lot and his family live, a great smoke rose from the plain. A hot, fiery smoke, as if from a furnace. I fear for their safety."

"What can we do?" I asked, leaning in toward Abraham.

"I will go find them," Ishmael said, lifting his head high.

I gasped. *Not my son.*

"No, son," Abraham said. "I have sent another to search for them. You must stay close. All we can do is pray that Jehovah will protect our family."

We knelt with him and Sarah and joined his prayers, begging Jehovah to protect Lot and his family.

Later, Ishmael and I climbed the hill and gazed toward Sodom. Flames rose high into the sky, sending smoke across the sky to fill our valley. I fell to my knees and prayed for Lot and Galya. She had been good to me in those early days when we first left Egypt. She did not deserve to die in such a raging fire.

Before the messenger returned, Abraham and Danil decided the grass on our hillside could no longer feed all our animals. We would need to move.

Ishmael helped pack our possessions and tent onto camels, and we traveled south once more. He had never moved and thought of our move as an adventure. I watched the sky, fearing we would feel Jehovah's wrath as Sodom and Gomorrah had. I did not want to burn.

The men found good pasture in the land of Gerar, between Kadesh and Shur. There, we set up our tents. We were now in the lands of Abimelech, a king of Canaan. Abraham warned us that once more, as in Egypt, Sarah's beauty would entice Abimelech. If he wanted her, she would have to go and she would need to tell the king she was Abraham's sister rather than his wife to protect Abraham.

Beauty? She is old. Her womb is dry. I gazed at Sarah, seeing clear, unwrinkled skin, clear eyes, and smooth, long hair. *In truth, she continues in her beauty, even in her old age.* I remembered her in the women's quarters of Pharaoh's palace. *She still carries herself as a beloved woman. She was beautiful because she is loved and knows it.*

Abimelech had many wives, but none had conceived a child. One of his messengers told Abraham that Abimelech hoped Sarah would conceive his child. Abimelech's messenger took Sarah from our camp to his palace. I expected her to take me along as her handmaid, but she left me behind to care for Ishmael and Abraham.

Although I reveled in time alone with my man, I worried for Sarah. Her hands covered her stomach when she thought no one watched. She had a glow about her as Senet did in Pharaoh's court, and had been sick on the road from Moreh. She carried a child. I could tell, even though her body did not show it yet.

I knelt in my tent after she left and prayed for her and her child, as I knew she had once prayed for me. *Forgive my doubt. Nothing is impossible.*

Surely Jehovah, who had finally given a promised child to Sarah, would not take it from her. Each evening before bed, Abraham, Ishmael, and I would kneel and beg Jehovah to protect Sarah. I always added the child in my heart. Abraham must not have known of it, for he did not add the child in his prayers.

After two weeks, Abimelech sent a messenger to our camp demanding that Abraham go with him to the palace. He kissed me and Ishmael goodbye and rode off with the messenger.

I prayed for his safety while I waited.

Later that afternoon, Abraham returned with Sarah riding on a beautiful white mare that Abraham had not taken with him.

"Abimelech gave her to me," Sarah said. "He gave us herds of sheep along with menservants and maidservants."

"Why would he do that?" I asked. Other women stayed near, waiting to learn what had happened.

"Jehovah came to Abimelech in the night and threatened to destroy him and his family if he did not send me away. I am Abraham's wife, not his sister. He gave me back to Abraham along with a thousand pieces of silver to atone for his sins and told us to choose a part of his land to live in."

"Did he ... did he try anything?" Bara asked.

"His wife, Sadiqe, took him to bed each evening. He never touched me, not even a chaste kiss."

I sighed with the other women at that.

"Their women have been barren. I pray to Jehovah each night that He will remove the curse from his women that they may give Abimelech many children."

That evening in our prayers, Abraham prayed for the women of Abimelech after thanking Jehovah for protecting his wife, Sarah, and their child.

There it was. She carried a child. My mouth dried and my stomach hardened. He would have a son by her, and mine would become second best.

Abimelech had given Abraham any part of his land that he wanted, along with all the other gifts, because he feared Jehovah's wrath when he took Sarah.

We packed our possessions once more while Abraham searched the land of Gerar for a new home. When he found a plain large enough to support all the animals in our herds, which he called Mamre, we moved there and set up our community once more.

Messengers arrived almost two months later. They gave us the news that Sadiqe and other women within Abimelech's household were with child. Jehovah had lifted his curse. Abraham, Sarah, Ishmael, and I knelt together to give thanks to Jehovah.

Sarah's days as a woman carrying a child within her were easier than I thought they would be. She had lost a child as a young woman and had never been able to conceive again. Now that her body was old and wrinkled, it easily adapted to the changes brought by the growing child.

After the first month of losing all her food, she soon adapted and never appeared to be out of breath or overtired from carrying the child within her.

It helped that Abraham called Yael's daughter, Liora, to serve Sarah. He feared she would lose this child if she did too much. However, the child had settled in her womb and would not leave it until time for his birth.

Three months after settling in Mamre, the man Abraham had sent to discover what had happened to Lot and his family returned. I was not invited to listen to the story, nor was I asked to serve them. They gave Liora that assignment.

Since Sarah had conceived, I was often excluded from family meetings, or I felt I was. This was one of those times when I was correct. Once more, I replayed my actions with Sarah and Abraham and those of Ishmael, trying to determine what we had done to be excluded.

Since they did not invite me, I rested in the shade of my tent near enough to hear the story the messenger brought. He told of a land that had once been green and vibrant, now devoid of all life. No serpents, lizards, or mice ran across the barren desert. Where there once had been a great city, no brick remained. Nothing that even suggested cities had once been located there.

I gasped and held my hand over my mouth. I had heard stories of the lush land near those cities. That was why Lot had chosen to live there. Now it was an empty desert.

"And Lot?" Abraham asked, his clothing rustling. I could almost hear him leaning forward, seeking for answers about his nephew. "Did you find Lot and his family?"

There was a pause. "Eventually. The small city of Zoar still stands. I asked about Lot there in Zoar. Men remembered seeing him on the day of the great fire. Men who ran to the walls that day to see the cause of the commotion lost their sight. Some blamed Lot. Others say he protected them from the great fire, for Jehovah loves Lot."

Abraham loved Lot. We had all begged Jehovah to protect his nephew.

"Perhaps Zoar was not destroyed because they took Lot in," Abraham said.

"What about Galya? Did the man you spoke to see Galya?" Sarah asked, her voice becoming unusually shrill.

There was another long pause. "No one in Zoar saw her. Lot had his two youngest daughters with him. None of the rest of his family. They left Zoar almost before the dust and smoke settled."

"No Galya?" Sarah asked, her voice only a little less shrill.

The messenger continued. Perhaps he shook his head. "After searching many days, I finally found Lot hiding in the mountains with his daughters."

"But Galya? What about Galya?" Sarah pressed. "Certainly he would not leave Sodom without his wife?"

"His wife is no more," the messenger whispered.

No more! My skin tingled.

"What happened?" Sarah exclaimed.

"Give him time to tell you," Abraham said. "Did Lot tell you what happened?"

"After much convincing, Lot finally shared. He did not want to speak of it and shuddered as he spoke. He was dirty and disheveled. He had not cleaned himself for many days."

I could understand that after such an experience.

"What did Lot tell you?" Abraham asked.

"He had visitors the night before the fire. Three holy men came to Sodom."

Was it the same who came to visit Abraham? The fire happened soon after.

"He tried to keep them out of the city, but they insisted on entering and went with Lot to his home. Lot locked the door behind them."

Smart man, if Sodom was as wicked as the stories I have heard.

"Lot made a feast for them. But the men of the city surrounded the house, seeking the visitors, desiring to know them."

The messenger stopped. He gulped his wine.

"They banged on the door and windows, calling for Lot to bring his visitors out so they could know them as they knew the other men in the city."

I silently gagged. *The stories travelers tell are true, then. It must have been horrible for Lot and Galya to live there.*

"Lot stepped outside to offer the men of the city his virgin daughters, rather than allow them to take his visitors, but they would not accept the exchange. They wanted the men. The men of the city would have crushed him, but one of the holy men opened the door enough to pull him inside."

Lot is a good man? How could he do this? He wanted to give his daughters to those awful men?

The messenger continued his story. "When the men of Sodom would not stop beating on Lot's door, the holy men afflicted them so those wicked men could no longer see to find the door."

"How did they escape?" Sarah asked.

"After Lot tried and failed to convince his sons, his daughters, and their husbands to leave with him, the visitors told him to leave the family and escape. Somehow, the holy men helped Lot, his wife, and his daughters to depart from the city. They were told to flee to the mountains and not look back. Lot argued with the visitor, fearing he could not live in the mountains alone. He convinced them to allow his family to go to Zoar."

Lot. He should have listened. I wiggled in my seat, hoping not to miss any of the messenger's story. My spinning lay unnoticed in my lap.

"And I tried to bargain for Lot's safety," Abraham said. "I begged Jehovah to protect him and his family if the holy men could find as few as ten righteous men. Sadly, they did not."

"Only one. Lot. Only he would leave Sodom. The great fire destroyed all the others. If there were any others, the fire destroyed them. Lot and his daughters hurried to Zoar, as directed by the holy visitors."

"But what happened to Galya?" Sarah asked in a plaintive voice.

The messenger paused before answering. "She turned to look back ..."

"And?" Abraham and Sarah asked at the same time.

I leaned forward, hoping to better hear his answer.

"A daughter walked behind her and saw. She turned back toward Sodom and ..." The messenger paused. I could hear him gulp wine. "She was turned to a pillar of salt."

For looking? Is Jehovah that cruel? My heart beat wildly.

"For disobedience?" Sarah said with a gasp.

"That is what the daughter told me," the messenger said.

When Abraham spoke again, his voice was shaky. "More than disobedience. She must have longed for the life she left in that city and wanted to return to it. Jehovah would not have punished her so intensely otherwise."

"She will be a warning to others for centuries," Sarah whispered.

A warning? More than a warning. Her heart must have been with her family in Sodom and longed to be with them. She will be.

"We must look forward to the good Jehovah has for us, not backward to the enticements of the Destroyer and the world."

I thought of Lot and the pillar of salt that once was Galya. How would Lot survive without her? Tears dripped down my face.

Isaac

During the middle months of Sarah carrying her son, the women of our village would come to me, questioning if she truly did.

"How can a woman of her age carry a child?" Adi asked. "Is she not well past the age to conceive?"

"I thought so, but nothing is impossible with Jehovah, it seems," I said.

"Jehovah blessed her?"

I lifted a shoulder in a small shrug. "It seems He has."

I helped Sarah dye some wool blue, and we wove blankets for the coming child as we had done in the time while we waited for Ishmael to be born. I helped other women sew clothing for the child.

Ishmael questioned me about Aunty Sarah. "Why is she getting fat?" he asked.

"She has a baby growing inside her."

"Did she swallow it?" Ishmael asked.

I laughed. "No. She and your father loved each other, and Abraham placed his seed within her."

Ishmael twisted his eyebrows. "Like when the rams ride the ewes?"

I giggled. "Yes, son. Much like that."

"I thought she was too old. If Aunty Sarah were a ewe, Danil would have slaughtered her long ago."

"But Aunty Sarah is a woman and your father loves her."

"Too bad," Ishmael said as he walked away.

How can you be so cruel? I shook my head. I had not raised a son to be unkind.

Abraham spent more time with Ishmael in the months between learning of Lot and Sarah's giving birth to Isaac. Abraham took my son with him when he took the sheep into the hills. Ishmael walked confidently ahead, calling to the sheep. Abraham had to be impressed by his abilities.

Ishmael always returned from spending time with his father full of energy and chatter. He told me about the sheep, the chipmunks, and other small animals, and the dangers they faced that day. I always enjoyed listening to him share, even though I feared what he faced in the hills. What would I do if a wolf found him alone, searching for his father's sheep? What would Ishmael do?

In the last month before Sarah was to deliver her child, I entered her tent to find her reading.

"What are you reading?" I asked.

"A book Abraham gave me, written by Eve. He thought it would better help me prepare for this birth."

A slight heaviness filled my chest. I would have liked to have read that before Ishmael's birth. I would love to read it now. "What have you learned?"

"Eve had only Adam to help her with her first children. No women like Bara to help her."

I inhaled, thinking of the day I birthed Ishmael. "Only Adam? How did he know what to do?"

She shook her head. "I do not know. Perhaps he learned from watching the animals. I appreciate Bara more now."

"Did you learn anything else about Eve from her book?"

"They faced challenges I never expected. I grieved with her when her children refused to follow the truths she and Adam taught them. They lost the blessings of Jehovah."

I nodded my head. I had learned of Jehovah's love and blessing in the years I had spent with Sarah and Abraham. I learned of His love when I ran to the desert before Ishmael's birth, among other times.

Sarah often expressed her concern that she would be embarrassed by her cries. "I do not want to shame myself," she would say.

Then, not many days before the pains in her womb began, she stopped fearing and spent the days with a smile on her face.

"What changed?" I asked.

"Abraham spoke to Jehovah and gave me a blessing."

I crunched my eyebrows together. "A blessing? What is a blessing?"

"Abraham set his hands on my head and said a special prayer. Through him, Jehovah told me I would deliver the child with no problems and our son will be born healthy."

"It must have been nice."

"Abraham would have blessed you, but he did not understand this until I read Eve's book. She received blessings from Jehovah before the births of her children."

"I would have liked one of those, before ..."

"I would have too, in the days when I lost my first child." Sarah's voice carried all the longing I felt.

A week later, Abraham woke me in the night. "I think Sarah would appreciate your help. Bara is with her, but you know what it is like to give birth."

I woke suddenly at his words. "Give me a moment to pull on my dress. Ishmael ..."

"... will be fine. I will ensure he eats before he goes to help the herders." His pinched face belied the calm of his words.

I kissed Abraham on the cheek and pulled a dress over my head. I slipped my feet into my shoes and hurried to Sarah's tent.

She lay in the bed moaning. I remembered the depth of those those pains and found her hand and held it as I rested on a stool next to her bed.

Bara nodded to me. "Dip the cloth in water and wipe her forehead. It will help her."

I remembered how much that helped me to cool and calm my emotions, and quickly followed Bara's instructions.

Sarah amazed me. Although she writhed in pain, she did not scream. She moaned and cried, and breathed deeply, controlling her pain. She did everything Bara suggested until, with one last big push, the child finally slipped out of her body into Bara's waiting hands.

Bara cleaned his mouth and rubbed his back. When the boy did not cry or gasp, she held him up by the ankles and slapped his buttocks. The child squalled.

"He lives, Hagar," Sarah cried. "I have a child. He lives and so do I. Thank Jehovah."

"Yes, Sarah. You have a son. Thank Jehovah."

And I am no longer the favorite. My stomach clenched. *My son is no longer the heir. Yours is. How will this change my life? How will it change Ishmael's life?*

Bara called to me to help clean the child. He was a fat, noisy child, a child of Sarah and Abraham. Bara wrapped him in a blanket we had woven before his birth and handed the baby boy to his mother.

While Bara taught Sarah and the babe how to nurse, I found a clean cloth and washed the blood from Sarah's legs.

"I must help her expel the afterbirth before we wash away the blood," Bara said as she massaged Sarah's stomach.

"That is right. I forgot," I said.

After she expelled the bloody mess, I cleaned her legs and belly while Bara took the afterbirth out to bury. She invited Abraham into the tent to see his son as she passed him.

He only had eyes for Sarah. She was his beloved. I was her handmaid and his concubine once more.

"I wanted to laugh that day, too," he whispered to Sarah. "I wondered how an old couple like us, long past the time of raising children, could ever have a child." He bent low and kissed her gently. "And now we have a son."

I cleaned the last of the blood from her legs and set a blanket across them.

"Isaac, as the visitor promised."

I picked up the bowl of bloody water and hurried from their space. They did not need me.

Eight days later, Abraham took Isaac to be circumcised in front of the men. I stayed with Sarah while Ishmael went with Abraham and Isaac. We chatted together about almost anything except what Abraham was doing to her baby.

I understood her feelings. Although other newborn boys joined in our camp since the commandment had come for men and boys to be circumcised, Isaac was her first son. We did not know what to expect. How would little Isaac handle his pain?

Bara had given Sarah an ointment to put on him to keep the cloth covering from sticking to his tender injury. We waited for Abraham to return with the baby boy.

We could hear Isaac squalling from a distance when Abraham and Ishmael returned with him. Sarah clenched her hands together, moaning softly.

"He did not cry until we left the men to return home," Abraham said. "I do not know why he is crying so much now."

Sarah unwrapped the child. He lay naked in the blanket. Dried blood stuck the blanket to where he had been circumcised.

"No wonder he cries," Sarah exclaimed with a frown. "You did not put any of the ointment on him, nor did you put a clean cloth over the injury."

"Should I have done that?" Abraham asked, his eyes widening.

"Did you not listen to Bara when she came?" Sarah asked as she carefully administered the ointment.

Isaac's screams became low whimpers. Sarah put the cloth over his bottom, dressed him, and wrapped a clean blanket around him. "There, there," she crooned. "Mama understands. It is hard to be a baby boy and have your father do that to you."

"I did it —" Abraham started.

Sarah lifted a hand to stop his utterance. "He only did it to you because Jehovah commanded it. Your father made a covenant with Jehovah and this is the evidence of that covenant you men must carry with you through time."

She finished wrapping little Isaac in a soft blanket and set him to her breast. He ate hungrily, his hurt almost forgotten, although he whimpered at her breast occasionally.

"You said that so well," Abraham whispered.

"It was lovely," I added. "It is good for our boys to know why we do this to them. Did you understand, Ishmael?"

Ishmael grimaced, remembering the day about a year earlier. "I understand. I am glad that is something I only have to do once."

Abraham tipped his head back and shouted with laughter. Sarah shushed him with a look, but his laughter continued.

"You are correct, my boy. I would not want to do that more than once myself."

Sarah and I laughed softly. We were not required to suffer that pain. Ours was different. We suffered through the hours of childbirth.

Sarah stayed within their tent caring for Isaac for forty days after Isaac's birth. I remembered how wonderful it felt to have those days to myself and Ishmael. At Sarah's age, she needed every one of those days to help her heal and prepare for the days ahead. Her son would soon become a busy little boy that ran with all the other boys.

The day after she left the tent and rejoined our village, the three visitors returned.

Since Sarah had a child to care for, I made the cakes for them. I brought them to Abraham and the holy men.

After they ate, one said, "We are here to meet your child, Isaac."

Abraham bowed at his waist and rose. He entered the tent and I left. I remained near the fire, tending our dinner, but still close enough to hear some of the conversation.

"Sarah should come out as well," one visitor called.

Soon I heard one say, "We are your servants. Worship Jehovah only."

Sarah must have fallen to her knees in front of them.

"You promised me a child," Sarah said, emotion filling her voice.

"We did."

"Here is the child, Isaac, you promised." She struggled to keep the quivering from her voice.

"He is as beautiful as we expected," one said.

"Will you laugh when Jehovah promises you blessings again?" another asked.

"No. I now know for certain that nothing is impossible for Jehovah." She sniffed back her tears.

"Remember this," a man said. "Tell your family so they will remember. Nothing is impossible. Jehovah can do anything he chooses."

I stirred the stew. I should not be listening in to the private conversations of Abraham and Sarah. I wanted to be part of their family, but they had not included me in this. A bitterness filled my throat. I had never felt this before. I swallowed hard, trying to get rid of it.

I walked to my tent and retrieved my spinning. I needed to do something and think of other things, not my loneliness.

As I spun, the refrain echoed through my thoughts: *I have Ishmael. I am not alone.*

Ishmael changed after Isaac's birth. Perhaps he heard me mention my concerns that he would no longer be Abraham's heir. Perhaps he was jealous of his little brother and the attention the baby received. I do not know. All I know is he changed.

Rather than lead his friends with laughter and fun, he stomped through the camp, shouting orders to the herders, and fighting with the other young men. I heard women whisper my boy had become a self-centered braggart.

I suspect he had. He wanted to prove to his father he was capable and would be an acceptable heir. When I watched Abraham with Isaac and Sarah, I had similar feelings. I wanted him to look at me like that again. I wanted him to remember that Ishmael was his son as well.

Abraham's attention was focused on the baby, not the young man. He spent time with his wife rather than his concubine. Envy crowded into my soul.

I passed Abraham's and Sarah's tent and heard her grumble rather loudly, "Hagar should control him better. She allows him to run wild."

I stopped and listened, wondering how Abraham would respond.

"He is my son as well," Abraham said. "I should be more strict with the lad."

"Lad? He is almost fifteen. He is a young man."

"Halfway there, I suppose."

He is nearly a young man. You should teach him to be a man. I shuffled my feet. *I should not be listening in to their conversation, even if they speak of me and my son.*

"He is old enough to go with the herders and order them about," Sarah screeched.

"I have heard him do that," Abraham said in a quieter voice. "I will talk to him."

I tore myself from their tent and hurried on to do more of my chores. I did not need to hear them argue about my son.

But Jehovah had promised Ishmael a large posterity. He would become a father of many nations. When he came to me the next day, I reminded him of the promises given to me. "Do you remember the promises the angel gave me when I carried you?"

"No, mother, I do not," Ishmael said, cocking one head to the side.

"The angel told me you would be a powerful man and the father of many nations."

"I remember that. I will be wealthy as well." He lifted his chin. "Father is wealthy. He is ancient already. As his first-born son, his wealth will come to me."

"No, son," I said, taking his hand. "Sarah's son will inherit. Isaac is the first son of the first wife."

"But I am his first son," Ishmael argued, and his eyebrows crowded together. "I will get more than him and have more power over our people."

"No, son. That is not the way it is. The law is that the oldest son of the first wife inherits before the oldest son of a concubine. You would have inherited if Sarah had not had Isaac."

Ishmael stomped his foot. "That is not right. I am the oldest. I should inherit."

"It is not fair," I agreed. "But that is the law."

"Father is the leader of the land. He makes the laws. He can change this law."

I shook my head. "He cannot change this law. It comes from Jehovah. It has been this way since the beginning of time."

Ishmael bent over and picked up a rock. He bounced it in his hand. "It is not right." He threw the rock and watched it rebound across the other rocks, then turned and ran to join his friends.

I turned to go to my tent and saw Sarah stride toward her tent, her face and shoulders tense.Had she heard Ishmael's complaint? That would not be good.

I heard him boast to his friends more than once, and his words hurt me. I hoped Sarah did not hear them. What would Abraham say if he heard Ishmael say such words?

"Just like old Sarah sent my mother away when she carried me, I will send Isaac away when Father dies and I am the master," he said one day.

Another day, he boasted, "Old Sarah is too wrinkled and old to be a mother. I feel sorry for little Isaac. Worse for him, he will become a herder for me, since he is the second son."

I reminded him of the truth. He would not be the master of all Abraham owned. Isaac would.

"No! Father will not allow that to happen to me," Ishmael shouted and ran out of the tent.

What would Abraham do if he discovered Ishmael's dissatisfaction? Would he explain it to my son?

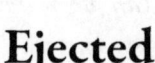

Ejected

O n the day Isaac was to be weaned, Abraham held a feast for all who lived in our household and all who lived close to us in the surrounding country. He ordered sheep and oxen slaughtered. The women stayed busy for a week baking cakes and breads and preparing other dishes.

I did not always see what Ishmael did as I worked to helped prepare, but I hoped Abraham would take a moment to speak with him.

On the day of the feast, everyone would sit at the table cheering little Isaac on as he drank milk from a cup and enjoyed many of the foods everyone else ate.

While waiting for the meat to finish cooking, Abraham laughed and talked with all the visitors from outside the camp. He boasted he had two righteous sons to follow Jehovah. He carried Isaac on his shoulders to supervise the men.

I saw Sarah talking with Bara across the clearing where we had set tables up. She pointed toward Ishmael and frowned. They spoke more and Bara pointed toward Abraham, who bounced through the camp with Isaac on his shoulders. What had Ishmael done this time? If Abraham would share more of his time with his first son, perhaps he would not misbehave.

At last, we all assembled at the table to watch little Isaac drink his milk and eat his food. Everyone laughed and cheered as he set his cup on the table.

Ishmael joined the other boys at a table, laughing and shouting. "I hope Isaac enjoyed nursing from his mother. He will not have her to protect him anymore. He will have to grow up now and learn how to be subject to me, his older brother. I will inherit. Isaac will get my left overs as I give my scraps to the dogs." He tossed fat from his meat to the dogs.

Beware, Ishmael. Sarah can be jealous and vindictive! I stepped toward him and furrowed my eyebrows.

But Ishmael did not stop. "He will wish he still nursed at his mother's teat."

Sarah rose to her feet. Anger filled her face and she pounded on the table. "That is enough! Isaac will not be your slave. He is Abraham's son."

Everyone remained in silent surprise.

"Ishmael," Abraham bellowed. "You will apologize to your Aunt Sarah."

Ishmael shoved his chair back and stood. His chair toppled over from the effort. He turned toward Sarah and opened his mouth. Nothing came out. I mouthed the words for him, 'I am sorry.' But his eyes locked on Sarah and he did not speak them. He turned on his heel and ran away.

Cold overwhelmed me. This would not be good. I could tell.

Sarah's face became redder than I thought possible. Redder even than that day I enticed her into the anger that chased me alone into the desert.

The guests overcame their stunned silence and began to eat and whisper among themselves once more.

Isaac took no notice of his mother's anger and continued to eat. The women surrounding Sarah enticed her to rejoin the celebration.

I feared it had not ended. My legs tightened in fear.

Late that night, after we had settled into sleep, Abraham scratched at my door.

"I am sorry, Hagar," he said when I opened the tent door. "Ishmael's behavior has become too difficult for Sarah and me. She has demanded that you leave with the boy."

I glared at him for a long moment. "You would send your son into the wilderness with no food or water?"

"I did not say that. I said you two must leave by sunset tomorrow. I took the matter to Jehovah. He agrees. It is best for Isaac and for Ishmael if you separate from us now."

"You would send away your son? Your first-born son? I thought you loved him!" I cried.

Abraham buried his face in his hands. "You know I love the boy, but he has become defiant." Pain filled his voice. He lifted his head and peered into my eyes. "He brags of things he will do when I die. We both know I am old and may not live until Isaac is old enough to take responsibility for my property."

"And me? What of me? Did you not care for me even a little?"

"It shreds my heart to send you and Ishmael away, not knowing where you will go or how you will survive. However, Jehovah has decreed it is to be so."

"Sarah decreed it and you listened!" My voice rose louder. "You always take her part and do what she says. Are you not the patriarch? Are you not the one to determine what happens within your home and among those who look to you as a leader?"

"Hagar, be still. You will wake the boy." Abraham set a hand on my arm.

"I will not be still," I said. My voice neared a scream. "You only care that others within your community will hear me and wonder at your leadership."

"No. Yes." He ran his hands through his hair. "But I do not want you to wake Ishmael. He will need his rest to travel tomorrow."

"You are accepting Sarah's will? You will send us away? Is there nothing I can do? No way Ishmael can beg for yours and Sarah's forgiveness?"

Abraham ducked his head. "He had his opportunity. He would not. It is done. Jehovah has determined this is best for us all." He lifted his head and rolled his shoulders back. "You and Ishmael will be blessed. He will lead a great nation, just as the angel who came to you long ago decreed. But it will not happen with you two living here. Ishmael's actions will lead to greater danger for both of the boys. It is better you leave tomorrow."

He is just a boy. He should have another opportunity to change. I lifted my hand and opened my mouth.

"No. You must leave tomorrow, before the sun sets."

Anger rose in me suddenly. My body became hot and my nostrils flared. I stepped close to him and I spoke in a low, dangerous tone. "I will not wait until tomorrow. We will leave now if we are so unwanted."

"Wait until dawn to leave. You will need to see the way to go."

"And which way is that?" I sneered. *Did he care where we went, what we would do to eat or drink?*

"That way." His arm pointed in a southwest direction. "You will find help if you travel in that direction. I will provide you with water and other assistance in the morning."

"If you must," I growled.

"Hagar," Abraham said, his voice becoming the loving man who had brought Ishmael into the world. *Now he acted like he cared for us? No!*

"Go!" I said, unable to hear that voice any longer. I turned my back to him. "If you wish," Abraham said. "I will return in the morning."

I said nothing more to him and he left my tent.

I spent the hours between then and dawn going through my possessions, frowning at each item. *Was this mine or Sarah's?* I hesitated. *I had been given to her as her handmaiden. Was anything beside Ishmael mine?* I chose a few things precious to me. I took a string of beads Abraham had given me when Ishmael was born, a shawl Sarah had woven and given me in celebration of Ishmael's second birthday, and a beaded bag Bara had given me.

I tucked some meat left from the feast the day before into my bag and filled two jars with water before I woke Ishmael.

"You must rise and dress quickly," I said.

He rubbed his eyes. "Father said the sheep would not go out until later today. Why are you waking me?"

"Your father has decreed that we must leave his camp. Because of the things you said about Sarah and Isaac, we are no longer welcome."

His face crumpled, then he stomped his foot. "I am his heir!" Ishmael shouted.

I set my hand over his mouth to quiet him. "No. You are not. On the day Isaac was born, you lost that privilege. You are second in line, and Jehovah will ensure that Isaac lives to inherit."

"But ... But ..." he spluttered.

"You did this to us with your bragging words. You could not keep your thoughts to yourself." I fought to keep my voice quiet. "You could not find the grace to welcome your brother to the family and wish him well, even though he displaced you. Abraham is a good man. He would have divided his property and given you enough to make you a wealthy man and sent you away with herders and bondsmen." I stared into his eyes. "You ruined it with your pride and foul mouth."

Ishmael cowered at my words. "I did not know."

"I told you to control your mouth. But you would not. We must leave. Now."

He opened his mouth, then closed it. "I will go beg Father to forgive me. He is a forgiving man."

"Do you not remember what happened to Galya? She looked back and was turned to salt! There is forgiveness and there is punishment. We have received punishment for your actions." I leapt up. "Now get up and be dressed before the sun has crossed the mountain peaks. We are leaving as soon as we can see to travel."

When we left our tent, Abraham waited there with bread and water for us to take on our journey.

"I would have brought you a donkey and other supplies, but you are leaving before I can gather them together," Abraham said.

"Father," Ishmael cried, plaintively. His eyes watered and he lifted his arms to embrace his father. "Will you forgive me?"

"I cannot. You would not listen to my directions. I asked you many times to consider your ways. You would not. Now, you must suffer for your actions. Go." He pointed to the southwest.

Ishmael tried to cling to his neck, but Abraham shook him off. "It is too late. You must leave."

"Thank you, Abraham, for giving me a son," I said. Heaviness filled my body.

He nodded and looked in the direction we needed to travel. He moved no more.

I took Ishmael by the hand and walked out of the camp.

Ishmael and I walked into the wilderness with our heads held high. Sarah would not know of the sorrow that filled us. Grief filled me. Perhaps not Ishmael. It did not take long for the boy to look forward to a new adventure away from the protective eye of his father. He had never been in the wilderness alone. He would learn.

Ishmael took a sip from his bottle of water.

"Do not drink that too fast. This is all the water we have," I reminded him.

"So? We can find more. There are wells," Ishmael said, taking another gulp.

"We do not know where the wells are. The wilderness is a dangerous place. Mostly because we do not carry enough water."

"Father would not send us out here to die," Ishmael said, taking another drink.

"Perhaps not, but he cannot control the wilderness. You do not know. You have not been out here."

"But you have."

Had I? I looked out in front of us, then off in the other directions. "I do not know this place. I have never been here. I do not know where the wells or springs are. Please do not drink all your water yet."

Ishmael sighed with a loud noise and put the stopper back in his water bottle.

I searched the wilderness for trees or bushes — anything that would show me where to go to find water. All I could see were rocks and hills and sand, along with a few desert plants that did not require as much water.

I bit my lip, closed my eyes, and said a silent prayer. "Help me know which way to go."

When I opened my eyes, I still did not know which way to travel, so I marched forward, trusting Jehovah to direct my feet.

The morning was cool and Ishmael enjoyed the trek, looking at lizards and pretty rocks, forgetting about the water. However, it soon warmed and he opened his water again.

"Take only a small sip," I reminded him. "This is all we have."

He tipped the bottle up and drank from it.

"Ishmael!" I said sharply. "Do not gulp the water."

"But I am thirsty," he whined.

"If you think you are thirsty now, wait until the day becomes hotter and you are out of water."

He laughed. "We will find water before we ours is gone. I trust you."

I lifted my eyebrows. "You trust me? A woman who has been caught in the desert sandstorm with no water?"

He lifted the bottle and took another gulp of water. "You found a spring then. You will find one this time."

"Or we will die."

"You were promised I would be the father of a great nation. We cannot die."

"We can if we drink all our water!"

Ishmael laughed. "You will find more."

My stomach hardened. He did not understand what had happened. He expected Jehovah to reward his dangerous actions. I shook my head and took the smallest of sips of water. Ishmael would need some of mine. I found a small rock and put it in my mouth.

His eyes widened. "Why do you do that?" he asked.

"It helps to keep away my thirst."

He twisted his face as he looked at me. "How? That does not make sense."

"Try it. It does."

He shook his head. Then, to humor me, Ishmael found a small stone and popped it into his mouth. "Dry. Dirty. No water." He spat it out. "Did not work."

"Leave it there longer."

"You do that," Ishmael said. "I will drink water."

"Not now!" I cried and took his water bottle from him. "You are careless with this. I will carry all the water."

"You will drink it all," he complained.

"Did you see me drink half a bottle of water? Did you see me put a rock in my mouth? I will not drink it." I strode away from him across the rocky valley.

Ishmael hurried to catch up.

It was not long before he teased me for water once more. "I will not drink so much. May I have my bottle back?"

I glanced at the sun. "It has not been half an hour. You can wait."

I rationed his water and drank less myself. We still had a bottle of water between us by the time the sun set.

We ate some of the bread and a bit of the meat, then took a small sip of water. I wrapped myself in my long shawl. Ishmael wrapped his cloak around him and we lay down to sleep.

"The stars are bright, Mother," Ishmael said in a sleep filled voice.

"They are. Perhaps because we can see them without the fires of the camp, they shine brighter."

"I like them," he said, and fell asleep.

The lack of sleep the night before and the effort to cross the wilderness had exhausted me. I closed my eyes and slept as well.

Wilderness

I startled awake to the sound of a water bottle opening and water gurgling from it.

Suddenly, I remembered. Ishmael and I were in the wilderness with only a little water.

I jerked myself up. "Ishmael! What are you doing?"

"It is morning. I am thirsty."

I grabbed the bottle from him and sloshed the water inside. More than half gone.

"Did you drink some of this last night?"

"I woke with my mouth dry and could not return to sleep." He lifted a shoulder and reached for the water bottle.

"This is all we have. You may not have more now."

"But I am thirsty," he whined.

I huffed out a heavy breath. "You will be more thirsty later when the sun rises high. Do you not remember what happened yesterday?"

He huffed and leaned back on his heels. "You will find more. Jehovah will not allow us to die."

"Do you think he will save you when you have been careless with the water we have?"

"He promised I would be a father of many." Ishmael frowned. "Do you not believe Jehovah can do anything?"

"Jehovah gave Sarah a child when her womb had dried. He can do anything when we are obedient. But will He if we are not careful with our supplies? Will he save us from our own folly?"

Ishmael pouted but did not attempt to take the water bottle from me. He knew I was right. Sarah and Abraham had received Isaac because they had obeyed and done everything Jehovah asked.

I gave him some bread and meat. There was little of it left.

How will we survive without food and water?

"We must go as far as we can before it gets too hot," I said, lifting my bundle to my shoulders.

"I do not want to go any farther. It is hot."

"And it will be hotter. We have no more water. We must find a spring and shelter, or we will not survive the heat."

He moved slowly, but he rose and prepared to go.

"Which way this time, Mother?"

I looked behind us where our footprints had snaked through the wilderness. "Not that way."

I said a silent prayer, begging Jehovah to show us where we would find protection and water. Then I turned back and pointed the direction we had traveled. "Come. We will travel this way."

"You are certain?"

"Yes. We must move now."

I marched across the wilderness. Ishmael trod behind me, less certain of our direction.

"I must drink," he whined less than an hour later. "The sun burns."

"Only a sip." I gave him the water bottle and he drank from it longer than he should.

"Ishmael! We will have no water if you drink it like that!"

"I am thirsty."

"You will be very thirsty if you drink it all."

I took a tiny sip. I wanted to be like Ishmael and gulp all the water from the jar, but I knew the consequences. I had been alone in the desert once before. Instead, I found another small stone and put it in my mouth, hoping it would help quench my desire for water.

It helped, but not enough.

I gave Ishmael a stone and he dutifully put it in his mouth and we marched out across the wilderness.

It was not long before Ishmael nagged me for another drink.

I held up the bottle and gently shook it. "It is almost empty. What will you do when it is gone?"

"Hope for an angel to come and show us where water is. Did it not happen once before?"

"It did, my son. But we cannot expect Jehovah to send an angel every time we are lost in the wilderness, especially when we are not careful with the water we have. You can wait."

We trudged through the wilderness until the sun settled above our heads, burning us up. We stopped to rest under a small bush while we ate the last of the meat, a bit of the bread, and drank a sip of the water. Ishmael could not stop at a sip and drank more.

I never deprived him of anything while he was younger. Abraham gave him everything he wanted as well. This one small thing, a big need to keep us alive, he could not, would not deprive himself. It was too late to think about depriving him of small things now.

I swished the jar gently. Not much water left. I prayed we would find water soon, but I feared Ishmael's demand and insistence that an angel would come would be a problem for us.

We waited for the sun to move across the sky a distance before we took one more small sip of water and stepped out into the wilderness once more.

What would we do? I searched the horizon for trees that would signal water but saw none. All I saw were small bushes, and they were far apart. They were so small they would not give us much shade.

"Mother, I thirst," Ishmael cried after less than an hour of walking.

"I do as well."

"Give me water or I will die."

I turned back toward him, kicking through the sand.

"You will die if you drink the last of it now. Wait a while."

We marched onward to the south and east. There had to be water somewhere.

Jehovah bless us. Help us find water and food.

There were no trees on the horizon, none near us, none far away. No birds. No big animals. Only mice and lizards. What would we do to live?

I did not know. I could only move forward, praying Jehovah would bless us. I had no other choice. Abraham would not come to my rescue this time. He had sent us away. Sent his oldest son away because Sarah had demanded it. Why would he allow her to send us away?

In my heart, I knew why. I would not want another woman's son to stay if he threatened my son in the way Ishmael had threatened Isaac. But would I have sent them away alone into the wilderness? I could not say.

Night came, bringing relief from the intense sun. Our skin burned from the heat, glowing red in the evening light. I had no ointment to relieve the pain, no water to soothe it. I took a small taste of our water and gave Ishmael a small sip and the last of the bread.

I lay beside my son, begging Jehovah to help us. Could a wandering tribe find us? Was there water near? How could we survive in a desert without His help?

I slept fitfully, dreaming of the burning sun and dragging Ishmael's dead body across the wilderness. I woke with a start.

No! Ishmael would not die. Jehovah had promised he would be the father of a great nation. That cannot happen if he dies.

I woke him and gave him another small sip of water before we moved on, using the light of the moon to see. Ishmael whined about his thirst, complained he could not see, and moaned about his tired feet and burning body. For a time, he walked beside me. He slowly dropped back, falling farther and farther behind. Near midday, I turned to find see him lying prostrate on the ground. I hurried back to him.

"Water," he moaned. "I need water."

I knelt next to him and gave him the last sip of water in the bottle. Without thinking, I tucked the empty bottle in my pocket as I took Ishmael by the hand and lifted him to his feet.

He plodded along beside me for almost another hour before falling behind again.

"Do not fall behind," I warned him when I returned to help him. "I cannot help you every time."

I put my arm around him and held him up as he stumbled. He mumbled something. I held him close, keeping him on his feet.

"We will find water. Stay with me," I said.

Ishmael could only mumble a response.

Eventually, he fell again.

I could not lift him to his feet. He lay mumbling incoherently.

I searched in all directions for a tree, a bush, a large rock, anything that would provide shade.

Low brush grew a short way from where Ishmael lay. Nothing else.

I took Ishmael under the arms, dragged him to the bush, and pulled him beneath it. A bit of shade would be better for him than laying in the blistering sun.

I bent to whisper to him. "I go to look for water."

Ishmael only mumbled something I could not understand.

I kissed his forehead and glared at the bleak landscape. Which way would be best to go find water?

A low hill rose in the south. I ran to it, hoping to see water on the other side. I scrambled to the top and peered in all directions, expecting to see signs of water.

All I saw was another low slope back to the east. Would there be water there?

I raced down the hill and across to this new knoll. How had I missed it in our trek? Had my head been too low, focusing on the next step?

I stumbled across the dry wilderness, tripping on something. I fell to the earth, sand filling my mouth. I pushed myself to my knees and spat out the sand. I had to find water for my son or he would die. I pushed off my knees and inhaled a deep breath. I could do this.

On I ran to the low mound, tripping and falling as I climbed it. Once more, I pushed myself to my feet at the top and gawked at my surroundings.

I only saw rocks and sand. Not even a bush grew. No travelers passed near or far. I slumped and shook my head. Perhaps I missed something?

Did Ishmael still live in this heat? I pulled myself up once more and ran to where I left him. I fell next to him, touching his neck and searching for the blood flowing through him. He still lived.

"Ishmael, I love you," I cried. "You must live. I have not found water yet, but I will."

I pushed myself to my feet and ran toward the mound in the south. Surely there would be water somewhere that I could see from there? A tree? A pool? A caravan? Something!

I kept myself upright as I raced up the hill, though more slowly than I ran the first time.

As I caught my breath, I gazed into the desert, seeking every shadow, praying for water, begging for help.

Nothing.

I must have missed something on the east slope. I would go look once more.

I hurried toward the east hill, falling to my knees once, scraping them. I could not waste this moisture. I licked the blood from my knees. It did not help.

Standing at the top of the eastern hillock, I wanted to cry. There were no shadows to investigate. No water to drink or give my boy. No travelers with food and water to help us.

I dragged my feet as I returned to my son. His chest still rose, but barely. When would Jehovah take him?

I bent and touched his face. He no longer mumbled. If I did not find water for him soon, I would be alone in this wilderness.

"Help me!" I cried. No tears leaked across my cheeks. I did not have enough water in me to form tears. I gawked into the sun-drenched sand. My only hope was the hill in the east. Perhaps travelers would travel by.

I ran to the south hill, and on to the east hill four more times, stopping to check on Ishmael on each return trip. I still saw no water. No travelers. No signs of help.

I needed help, someone, somehow, I must find water. I could not live without my son.

I stopped to examine Ishmael one last time. He still lived, but only barely. I had to find water for him.

As I stumbled up the hill to the south, I begged Jehovah to help me find water. There was still no hint of it.

One last time, I went to the eastern hill. There had to be water. I could no longer run. I trudged through the hot sand, barely able to move. Still no water.

I returned to Ishmael. His chest barely moved. He would die if I did not find help. But I had done everything I knew. I had searched. I had prayed. What more could I do?

I moved away from Ishmael, about as far as he could shoot his arrows, and sat in the sand. "I do not want to see my son die," I wailed. "Jehovah, help us. I have done all I know to do to keep us alive. Only Your help will save us."

I set my head on my knees and sobbed, with no tears falling from my sun-dried eyes.

Saved

I did not want to see my son die. Something told me to look up. Still, however, I gazed at the shrub where I had left him. A man, no, an angel, stood beside him.

I wearily tromped to where the angel waited, unsure if he was real. Relief flooded my soul when he spoke.

"What is your problem, Hagar?" he asked. "Fear not. Jehovah has heard your cries and the voice of your son. Lift him up. Jehovah will yet make of him a great nation."

I stared dumbly at the angel, unable to comprehend his message. "How can that be? We have no food and no water. We will die here in the desert without them."

The angel dug his heel into the sand and water seeped into the indentation. Water where none had been! A flutter rippled through my stomach. I bent to gather the water before it disappeared back into the sand, pulling the empty bottle from my pocket.

I filled the bottle and gave water to Ishmael, dripping it onto his lips with the cloth from my pocket. I tipped a little onto his lips, then tipped more on the linen cloth and dampened his face.

Only then did I bend to refill the bottle and drink of that water. It tasted heavenly. I bowed at the angel's feet.

He lifted me up. His touch filled me with love. "Do not worship me, for I am a servant of Jehovah. You will live and the boy will grow and become a great nation. Trust Jehovah."

Trust Jehovah. Yes. He always comes when I have done all I can, when hope is almost gone.

I bent to refill my bottle of water. When I lifted my head once more, the angel had left. But water continued to seep from the small place where he had dug his heel into the sand. I set rocks around it to keep it from flowing away.

We had water. We would not die of thirst.

I dripped more water onto Ishmael's lips from my cloth until he licked his lips. Finally, he opened his eyes.

"Mother, you have water?"

I wanted to cry, but I did not want to waste my precious moisture. Instead, I nodded.

"An angel came while you slept," I said.

"I told you Jehovah would not let us die." He rose and gawked at the water. "It overflows."

I turned my gaze to the water. The little indentation had filled and had covered the rocks I had placed surrounding it. I removed the rocks and set them out a distance from where they were earlier.

Three more times the water overfilled the space, and I had to move the rocks outward before the water slowed and stopped overfilling the new spring.

Ishmael drank his fill, as I had. We sat together beside the spring and offered prayers of thanks to Jehovah.

After an hour, Ishmael rubbed his stomach. "I am hungry. Do we have food?"

"We ate it all yesterday. I am hungry too."

I dug into my pocket once more, hoping to find food I had missed. I found five dates. I gave one to Ishmael and ate another. I kept the others back, not knowing when we would find more food. My date tasted heavenly.

We talked about what to do.

"Now what do we do?" Ishmael asked.

"A good question," I responded. "Should we leave the spring and seek another home or stay there near the spring where we knew we would have water?"

"We have had no water for so long."

"Where else will we find water? We cannot expect the angel to return every time we thirst unto death." I shuddered at the memory of Ishmael lying under the bush, waiting for him to die.

"We have no food here," he said, eying my pocket.

"And if we eat what we have, we will have none anywhere." I shoved my pocket behind me.

"I am still hungry."

"You will be hungrier if we eat all the food we have."

Ishmael squatted in the sand in front of me with downcast eyes and a frown.

"We should pray about this tonight and decide tomorrow," I said. "We may find food."

We slept well that night beneath the bush near the new spring.

The next morning, I gave Ishmael another date.

"We have one more date," I said. "What will we do for food if we stay here?"

A bird circled the sky above us before it dropped to drink from the spring. Another bird followed it.

"I can catch birds to eat. Can you start a fire to cook them?" Ishmael said.

"How will we entice more birds if you kill them?"

"I will not kill all of them, just one today."

When the birds leapt to fly away, Ishmael jumped forward and caught the last bird.

I started a fire while he cleaned it.

We set the bird over the fire to cook and built a shelter to keep the sun off our heads from the dead brush that lay on the ground. It was small, but it protected us as we huddled beneath it in the heat of the day.

Ishmael formed a thin rope from the sinews of the bird and the fibers of a plant. With this, he made a trap.

During the night, small animals came to the spring to drink. A rabbit stepped into the trap.

It fed us the next day.

Over the following days, Ishmael caught birds and small animals to feed us.

Birds flew in to drink the water, leaving seeds behind. Date palms and other plants grew from these seeds.

We separated the spring, keeping a part of it clean for us to drink and a part for the animals.

I scraped the skins of the rabbits and other small animals and eventually created a small tent to live in with the feathers and skins. It was a colorful patchwork tent, but it provided us with protection from the weather and a place to call home.

Ishmael and I lived alone for nearly a year.

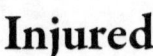

Injured

There were no crocodiles in the wilderness, but I often heard the roar of animals that sounded much like Grandfather Crocodile. Usually it was a lion. I finally learned to recognize them. Every time a lion would roar, I shuddered at the memory of my lost brother.

Ishmael learned to hunt the wild animals and soon we no longer ate only the small animals and birds that came to our spring.

After almost a year of living near the spring, we saw dust rising behind the hill to the east.

"What is that?" Ishmael asked.

"It could be anything." I started toward the hill, my heartbeat increased. Was it animals we could harvest or people?

"You are going alone?" Ishmael asked, running to catch up with me.

"Not if you go with me. But no one will know I am here alone if I stay low on the hill. I will be safe if you want to continue cleaning that antelope."

Ishmael glanced back at the antelope he had killed early that morning. Then he stared at the dust over the hill. "I would like to see what is crossing the valley on the other side of the hill. I will go with you."

We climbed the hill, dropping to our knees as we neared the top to shield us from view of whatever was out there. We did not know what we would find. It could be a herd of animals or a traveling caravan.

I lifted my head over the rise of the hill and peeked out. A group of people rode in a line on camels. A caravan! They rode purposefully forward, coming ever closer to our little valley.

"What brought them here after all this time?" Ishmael asked.

I could only shake my head. In all the time we had lived there, only birds and small animals had ventured to drink from our spring.

Ishmael and I scooted down the hill and hurried back to our tent and spring. We remained in front of our tent when the travelers rode toward us.

The leader pulled his camel to a stop and had it kneel so he could climb off.

"Peace be to you," he said. His eyes wandered from me to Ishmael, then around our little camp.

"Where is your man?"

"I am here," Ishmael said, standing tall. "I protect my mother while we await the return of my father."

"And who is your father?" the man asked.

I smoothed my dress. "Who are you?" I asked, stepping in front of Ishmael.

The man bowed his head. "I am sorry. I forgot my manners. I am Asad, the leader of this caravan. We are the tribe of Jorhom."

"How did you find us?" Ishmael pushed me aside and stood beside me. "No one has come this way for many days."

"There has never been a reason to come this way until now. We saw birds flying over us and led us here."

I peered upward. Birds flew in and landed near our spring, dipping their beaks into the cool water.

"I suppose they would lead you here."

"They did." Asad peered at our camp. "You have an unusual tent."

"We —" Ishmael said.

"— like it," I said, giving him a stern look. *We do not know this man. I do not trust him, yet. There are many more of them than us.*

"Made of rabbit furs and antelope skin?" Asad asked.

"And feathers. They gave their lives so we could live. We honor them by using their covering to cover us." I bowed my head. "Thanks be to Jehovah."

"Thanks be to Him," Asad responded. "May we water our animals?"

Does he truly worship Jehovah? I will watch him.

I looked at all the camels, dogs, sheep, and donkeys. Would our little spring support them?

He eyed me. "Your spring is small. We will bring one at a time. Will that work?"

"Until we enlarge the spring," Ishmael said.

Asad nodded to his people. One at a time, they dismounted and led their camels to the spring. The animals stayed out of the water, keeping clear. I watched closely, wondering if they would drink the spring dry.

After each camel drank, the spring bubbled up, refilling the section we had set aside for animals. After a little more than an hour, all the animals had drunk their fill and moved away.

The men brought out food for the animals and hobbled them away from the spring. The women brought out grains and honey, dried fruits and vegetables, and other foods I had not eaten for almost a year.

We had been alone for so long, my body quivered. I no longer knew how to be with others. Would they find me strange? Would I be acceptable to them? My mouth watered at the sight, but I said nothing to them as they lit a fire, dipped water from the spring, and prepared a thick soup.

"We would share with you," Asad's wife, Salwa, said. "You have shared your water. We will share our food."

I ducked my head in thanks. "We have antelope we can share."

"That will add to the soup," Salwa said.

I retrieved the antelope Ishmael had killed that morning and cut it into small pieces before adding them to the soup.

"Why are you here alone?" Salwa asked.

"Jehovah brought us here about a year ago," I said, not wanting to share the cause of our expulsion from Abraham's home camp.

"And your husband ...?"

"Abraham."

"Ah. You are his missing concubine."

My eyes opened wide. She had heard of me? "Hagar."

"Yes. That is the name I heard. We heard you left their camp with your son."

I nodded. They could think that. "Abraham brought us here because Jehovah commanded it. We have been blessed."

"I see," Salwa said as she stirred her soup.

She did not see, but she did not need to understand or know. That was my story. Mine and Abraham's. And Sarah's.

By the time the men had all the animals bedded down, the other men pitched their tents in a circle away from mine. The soup had cooked, and we all sat down to eat.

Salwa noticed I had no bowls or spoons for me and Ishmael and shared hers with us. She asked no questions of us. Perhaps she did know.

Asad and Salwa and their tribe stayed with me for almost a month. We shared news and stories. It took a few days to find comfort among so many people after being alone for so long. Ishmael led the men on a wildebeest hunt when dust rose on the other side of the east hill. They returned with enough meat to feed everyone.

When they left, the men left an extra tent for Ishmael and me to use.

"Your feather and rabbit fur tent will keep you warm," Asad said. "But this is larger. It will help to shield you from the heat of the wilderness."

Before they packed up their camels to move on, Salwa and the other women opened their bags of food and shared with me.

"Where will you go from here?" I asked.

"We travel toward Egypt," Asad said.

"My home," I whispered. "If you see a young woman who would make a good wife for my Ishmael, one who will follow Jehovah, invite her to come be his bride."

"You would do that?" Salwa asked.

"Do what?" I asked.

"Invite an unknown woman into your home?"

"Ishmael needs a wife. Yes. I would do that."

"Would you allow us to settle here with you?" Asad asked.

Would we? We had enjoyed life alone. But having others near had changed us. Could we live alone again?

"I will think about it while you are gone. When you return, I will have my answer."

Salwa hugged me before climbing onto her camel. "It is good to know you, Hagar. We will bring a wife for your son."

As the caravan left, Ishmael took my hand. "You would do that for me?"

"Do what?"

"Find me a woman to be my wife?"

"Yes, son. If you are to be the father of a great nation, you will need a wife."

Ishmael kissed me on the cheek, then danced away, whooping and shouting.

I grinned. I loved to make him happy.

One night, about a week after Asad and his tribe left us, Ishmael and I woke up to the roar of a lion in the distance.

I remembered the roar of Grandfather Crocodile. I pulled the blanket over my head. "Is the door closed tight?"

"Mother," Ishmael teased. "You do not think a thin skin door will keep out a lion?"

"It may."

"Or it may not. I will go out tomorrow and see why the lion roars."

I grabbed his arm. "It roars because it hungers. You will become his dinner."

Ishmael laughed. "Perhaps. I will see. When the sun rises, I will leave to find it."

"You cannot marry if you are dead."

"I will not die. Jehovah has blessed me. He will continue." He removed my clutching fingers from his arm. "Do not fear for me, Mother."

I could not settle the fear in my heart. What would I do if the lion hurt him? I had no ointments or bandages to heal him. Nor could I prevent his actions.

"Be extra careful."

I heard the smile in his voice. "Of course."

I woke before the sun rose the next morning and peered toward Ishmael's bed, as I always did.

My heart skipped a beat.

Ishmael was not there.

I leapt out of my bed and hurried outside, hoping he had gone out to relieve himself. My heart pounded as I called for him. But he did not respond. I searched the tent and found his weapons gone.

He went lion hunting. Alone.

I fell to my knees and begged Jehovah to protect my son.

The sun rose. When it burned my skin, I sought the shelter of the tent, sitting in the doorway where I could watch for Ishmael to return. As I waited, I murmured prayers to Jehovah. Surely, he would protect Abraham's son. He had made promises.

I stepped from the tent door long enough to prepare a simple meal. Ishmael would be hungry when he returned. I moved the food to the edge of the fire and returned to my place near the door, waiting and watching for my son to return. Jehovah would protect him. He had to!

The sun had passed its zenith before Ishmael's form smudged the horizon.

Jehovah be praised. He lives.

I wanted to rush to meet him, but Ishmael would not like me to fawn all over him. Instead, I went to the fire and made bread to go with the stew I had cooking.

"Mother!" Ishmael called as he neared their tent. "Mother, come see!" He had left me before to hunt, and always his voice assuaged the fear that gripped my heart. It released the pain this time as well.

I pulled the bread from the fire before I turned toward him. He had tied his cloak between two poles.

"What did you get?" I asked, pretending not to care, grateful he had returned home safely.

Ishmael flipped the cover off the lion. "This is the lion that roared outside our tent last night."

I gasped.

Ishmael pulled the biggest male lion I had ever seen from his dragging frame. "He put up a fight, but I was stronger."

I lifted my eyebrows. "You were stronger than him? How did you do this?"

He bent down and turned the lion so I could see. "I shot him in the heart. He saw me and raced toward me, determined to eat me. I pulled three arrows from my quiver and shot them one after the other into his heart. He slid to a stop at my feet. Dead."

"At your feet?" I said with a shudder.

He nodded. "At my feet. His hot breath warmed my face. The dust sprayed onto me. And he fell."

I fell to my knees. "Thank you, Jehovah."

Ishmael knelt next to me. "You did not need to fear. Jehovah was with me. He guided my arrows."

I rose and circled the gigantic lion, running my hands over his soft pelt, amazed that my son had killed this magnificent animal. "What will you do with this?"

"I will make a gown for my bride from this. Will you help me design it?"

I looked at the big lion once more. He had a beautiful skin. "Yes. This will make a beautiful dress for your bride."

After he ate the food I had prepared for him, Ishmael took the lion to the edge of the camp to skin it. He saved the sinews, claws, and teeth before he dragged the meat and bones into the desert for the jackals to eat. We had been taught not to eat the meat of predators.

Over the next weeks, I helped him design and sew together a lion skin dress. It was beautiful. I did not know if it would fit the woman Asad would bring from Egypt for Ishmael to marry.

Then one day, we heard another lion roar. I looked at Ishmael. "Do you want to hunt him?"

"I do. I want robes for me to match the gown for my bride."

I swallowed the sudden fullness in my throat. "We need to pray."

Ishmael knelt on the antelope rug in our tent. I joined him in his prayers for safety in his hunt the next day.

When we finished, my heart burned. I knew Jehovah would protect my son.

"Be safe, son," I said before we went to bed that night.

Once more, I woke to find Ishmael gone the next morning. I spent my time praying for Jehovah's blessing on my son throughout the day. When Ishmael did not return before the sun set that evening, I fell to my knees, begging Jehovah to protect my son.

Late that night he finally appeared from the dark, dragging a lion's skin with the sinews, claws, and teeth rolled inside. "This will make me a nice cloak," he said.

In the firelight, I saw deep, bloody claw marks on his chest. "You did not stop him before he reached you." I shuddered as I ran my fingers down the slashes. "How did you kill it?"

"She protected her litter of kits and refused to give up," Ishmael said. "Even with arrows in her heart, she fought for her babies. I finally had to beat her on the head with the hilt of my sword, as she was too close for me to shoot another arrow into her. It took time, but she finally died."

A lioness? With babies?

"What did you do with her babies?"

"They could not live without their mother. I took them by the scruff of their necks and slit their throats. I have enough pelts now for a blanket for you, as well as a cloak for me to match the dress we made for my bride."

I ran my hand through the soft pelts. The cub pelts were larger than I expected. Tears leaked from my eyes as I thought of the small family of lions now before us.

I turned my thoughts to Ishmael's injuries. Lion scratches had caused sickness in men. I washed the scratches in cold water while I waited for more to boil. When it bubbled, I dipped my cloth into the hot water and washed the scratches once more.

I had no ointment from a healer, but Ishmael had recently found a beehive. I dipped my finger into the honey and smeared it across his injured chest.

During the night, I heard Ishmael rolling and moaning in pain. When I touched his face, it burned. I dipped water from the spring to cool his face and body. Then I washed his scratches and smeared more honey on them.

In the early morning light, I saw streaks of red running up his body. I hid my fear and cleaned the scratches and smeared them with honey once more. He slept as his body worked to heal the sickness caused by the lioness's scratches.

I watched over Ishmael for three days, washing his scratches and smearing honey on them. I prayed between my ministrations, begging Jehovah to heal my son.

Finally, his body cooled and he awoke. He insisted he had healed enough to be busy with the sewing of his cloak and rose from his bed. Now, after he had healed, I fought off the tears that welled up behind my eyelids.

He did not move far from the entrance to our tent for the next week. However, in that time, he cut and stitched his cloak together and prepared the skin to make me a blanket.

Celebration

As we waited for Asad to return with a wife for Ishmael, he watched herds of antelope and wildebeest pass by us, searching for water. They did not smell our little spring and did not divert into our camp, for which we were grateful.

Ishmael went to the edge of the hill and his arrows found the hearts of three wildebeests who moved on the edge of the herd. After cleaning these animals in the wilderness and leaving the entrails for the scavengers to eat, he dragged the bodies to our camp.

While we smoked the meat, I scraped the hides and helped Ishmael make a smooth leather. He used these to make a new tent for himself and his wife. We were certain Asad would return with a woman soon.

After many weeks of waiting, Asad and his tribe returned from their travels to Egypt. Ishmael struggled to wait for them to ride toward our home.

We lingered together in front of my tent, waiting and watching. He had grown into a sturdy, tall young man, looking much like his father, although his brown beard had not filled in like Abraham's yet. His shoulders had broadened, with stronger arms and legs. Even with all his adult looks, the little boy surfaced as he waited, rocking back and forth on his feet, and struggling to stand still.

"Do you think Asad brought me a wife?" Ishmael asked.

"He said he would try to find a woman who would come be your bride."

We watched for a while longer.

"Will she be as beautiful as you?" he asked.

I blushed. "I hope so. Not all women are beautiful. Some are not so pretty on the outside and beautiful inside. Others are beautiful on the outside and have ugly, cranky, horrible actions. We will have to see."

"I would rather have a beautiful wife who is kind."

I took his hand and squeezed. "That would be nice. You want a gentle woman, one who is intelligent and able to survive in our wilderness home. That is most important. What good is a beautiful woman who whines about missing the city and who cannot cook or clean, weave or sew? How would you survive if she cannot heal your injuries?"

"True. But I still want a beautiful woman."

I smiled. Ishmael was still young. He would soon learn what made a woman beautiful.

Asad stopped his camel in front of our tent. "You have been busy. When I left, you had only one tent. Now you have two."

"We have been busy," I said. I nodded toward Ishmael. "My son has done much to prepare for a wife." I swallowed at the dryness in my mouth.

"It is important that I have a home prepared to welcome a woman," he said.

Asad nodded. "True. It is important to have a home for your new wife. If only you had a wife."

Ishmael groaned.

Asad motioned to one of his men to bring a camel forward. At his signal, the camel knelt. The man stood on the camel's leg to help a woman step down from the seat. She wore a veil across her face.

Ishmael sucked in a breath. "Is this ..."

"It is."

I breathed once more. I feared Asad had not brought a woman for Ishmael.

Ishmael stepped forward and took the woman's hand from Asad's man, helping her step away from the camel. He led her a short distance away from us, speaking softly to her.

We watched them talk together. I heard the familiar cadence of a woman from Egypt I had not heard in the many years I had been with Abraham and Sarah. I had to bite my lip to keep the tears back. *Home. Mother. My friends. No longer part of my life.*

Finally, Ishmael led the woman to meet me.

"Mother," Ishmael said. "This is Zulfa. She agreed to come into the wilderness to meet me. Now, she has agreed to become my wife." He looked at his feet. "How do we do that?"

My grin slipped. I had not thought of the rite needed to make them man and wife. Abraham performed it for the people of Mamre. How would I let him know we needed him now? He had not come to visit us.

"Jehovah will provide," I whispered.

"Your father will come," Asad said.

My heart leapt.

"How do you know this?" Ishmael demanded.

"We spoke to him as we returned from Egypt. He wanted to find you and your mother. We told him how to find you. He will come."

Ishmael bowed his head. "We will wait."

Zulfa was a pretty little girl, not much older than my Ishmael. She fit beneath his arm. She had swept her long, dark hair up to keep the sand out during her ride. She wore clothing like those of the Jorhom tribe: colorful, thick robes woven from camel hair.

Asad instructed his tribe to dismount. Soon, tents sprang as if from the ground. Fires glowed and delicious aromas of cooking food filled the air.

I brought out dried wildebeest and added the fragrance of a stew to the fragrances filling the air. Zulfa joined me at the fire, wanting to help.

I welcomed her to my fire with a brief embrace. "This time, you are the guest. I will share my tent with you until Abraham comes to marry you to my Ishmael."

Ishmael carried her trunk and basket of belongings into my tent. Zulfa disappeared for a time. When she returned, she was dressed in a simple linen shift. I had not seen one of those for many years. A tear traced the line of my face.

"Why do you cry?" Zulfa asked.

"I have missed the clothing of Egypt. I wore a shift like that one as a young girl."

"You are from Egypt?"

I nodded. "I came from Egypt. I no longer live there. I will not go there again."

I told her my story while the stew cooked. Her lovely dark lashes swept tears from her deep brown eyes.

"It was good for me to leave," I said. "I learned to love and worship Jehovah, and I have Ishmael. Soon, you will join our little family and we will grow."

Zulfa nodded. "My life was much like yours. Palace guards stole me from the streets as I went to the market for my mother. I have not seen her for many months. When Asad came to the palace searching for a wife for the son of Abraham, Nabukha brought me to Pharaoh. I had been hiding in an empty room since his favorite wife discarded me. She thought Pharaoh looked at me. If he did, I did not desire him in return. He is an old man, and I am a young maid."

"You were happy to leave Pharaoh's palace and the women's quarters?" I asked. I did not want to leave, but it had been good for me.

Zulfa lowered her eyes. "I miss my mother and father and my brothers and sisters. But I would never see them again, anyway. I am happy to be here."

Two days later, as we finished our morning meal, one of the Jorhom guards cried out a whistled warning. The men hurried to get their weapons while the women found places to hide from danger. With our hearts beating rapidly, Zulfa and I hid in my tent together until Ishmael came for us.

"Mother, Zulfa, come out," he said, fighting back the excitement. "You will want to meet our visitor."

"Visitor?" I asked, brushing back my hair.

"Come. You will see."

We walked from the tent and into the sun. Abraham visited with the men of Jorhom.

"Hagar," Abraham cried. He opened his arms to me.

I had not seen him in all the time since we left Mamre after Isaac's feast. Still, my heart overcame the outrage I felt that day. I hurried to him and fell into his arms. "You are here. I thought you forgot us."

He held me tight and nuzzled my hair. "I have not forgotten you. I have watched you from afar. Asad told me he found you here. He told me of the mission you sent him on. I waited until Jehovah told me to come visit you again. He says you have joyful news for me."

"Ishmael does," I said.

Abraham turned with me still under his arm. "Ishmael? What news do you have for me?"

"I need you to perform the marriage rite." He brought Zulfa from behind him. "This is Zulfa. She has agreed to be my wife."

Abraham stared at her for a long moment before grinning. "You are welcome to my family, Zulfa. I will be happy to perform the rite." He pulled her and Ishmael into a long embrace before releasing them. He put his arm around me once more and walked with us to the eating fire near my tent.

"When would you like me to perform this rite?" Abraham asked Ishmael.

"How long will you be here?" Ishmael asked.

"Until tomorrow morning."

"Could you perform the rite this afternoon?"

Abraham gazed at Zulfa. "Will that give you enough time?"

"I have nothing to wear for a marriage rite. I left Pharaoh's court with few possessions. Certainly, nothing to wear for a marriage rite."

"I can fix that," I said, gesturing for her to follow me to the tent. "Ishmael has prepared a dress for you. I hope you will like it."

We entered my tent, and I pulled out the gown we had made from the lion's pelt.

"This is so soft," Zulfa exclaimed. "How did you get this?"

"One night, after Asad left to find you, we heard a lion outside our camp. Ishmael went out the next morning and killed it before it could kill us. Later, he killed another lion and her cubs. We worked together to make this gown for you to wear."

Zulfa slipped out of the robes she wore to protect her from the sun and put on the lion gown. "It fits me perfectly."

"Amazing," I said. "We did not know how big or tiny you would be, yet we sewed this exactly to fit you."

She ran her hands down her sides. "This is so soft. I thought it would be heavy."

"And it is not?" I asked.

"No. It feels like my skin."

She dug through her basket and brought out a set of black beads.

"Beautiful," I cried, thinking of the beads my own mother wore.

The women of Asad's tribe prepared a feast for us. One brought in a crown of dried flowers to set on Zulfa's head.

When all was ready, I left Zulfa in the tent while I returned to Ishmael and Abraham.

Asad and his tribe gathered in the open space near the center of the encampment. When everyone had gathered and all prepared, I returned to the tent for Zulfa, leading her to the front of the crowd.

The women released a collective sigh and Zulfa ducked her head, blushing. Ishmael rose and took her hand.

"The dress looks beautiful on you," he whispered.

"Thank you," Zulfa murmured.

Abraham rose, and the two young people stood in front of him. He spoke sacred words that joined them as a couple.

I watched, allowing tears of joy to flood across my face. I had not lost a son. I reminded myself I had gained a daughter.

I did not think we would have sweet cakes or other special treats to celebrate the marriage. But Salwa and her friends had prepared sweet cakes in the days while we waited for Abraham to arrive.

We enjoyed a feast and celebrated long into the night. Early in the evening, Ishmael took Zulfa to his tent, which he had moved far away from the others.

As the feasting ended, Abraham took me to my tent.

"We have not been together for so long," I protested. *What will Sarah think?*

"You are still my wife. I have missed you."

"You missed me? You have Sarah and Isaac to keep you company." I tried not to reveal my bitterness.

Abrahan undid the pins from my hair and ran his hands through it. "I have missed you, Hagar. Sarah has missed you. You are our family."

"Yet you sent us away," I whispered.

"I did not want to do that. Sarah repented soon after you were gone, but Jehovah had agreed. It was best for you and Ishmael to leave my home."

"It is best for us to thirst in the wilderness? Best for me to almost lose my son to the sun and lack of water?"

"Jehovah promised he would care for you. He did. Look. You have water where there was none."

I wanted to pout. "No thanks to you. Jehovah sent an angel who found water for us."

"Jehovah cared for you."

I breathed out a deep breath. "He has. We would not be here still and Ishmael would not be married if Jehovah had not protected and blessed us. Ishmael killed the antelope and wildebeest for this tent. Birds led Asad and his tribe to us. They brought us Zulfa to be Ishmael's wife. Jehovah has provided for our needs."

"All praise to our loving Father and Jehovah, His son," Abraham said.

"I honor him each day."

Abraham sat in the dark on my bed. "Come, Hagar. Let us be together this one night."

I could not stop my tongue. "Will Sarah mind?"

"Sarah will mind, as you mind when I am with her. It is the way it is."

I slowly untied the ties that held my dress together at the shoulders and allowed it to fall in a heap at my feet before joining Abraham in my bed.

The next morning, Abraham kissed me. "I am an old man, but I will come when I can to help care for you."

"Ishmael and I are doing well alone. And now Asad and his tribe plan to join us."

"I know. I will not come often, but I will come to ensure that all is well with you and our son."

We walked into the early morning sunlight together. I prepared a small meal to break our fast, and some food for him to take with him in his pocket.

Ishmael and Zulfa appeared the next morning in time to tell Abraham goodbye. Abraham hugged Zulfa and shook hands with Ishmael, offering him a few words of wisdom. He then pulled me into his arms.

"I will miss you, Hagar. You have done well for yourself here near this spring. Trust Jehovah. He will care for you." Abraham kissed me then climbed into his saddle. "Farewell, my family. Be safe."

Abraham rode away, out of our little valley.

I was alone again.

There were no crocodiles here in this valley, but I heard them roar. I shuddered.

Jehovah, keep us safe.

Family

I did not see Abraham often in the next years. He was too old to travel the distance from Mamre to our little valley we called Paran.

After Abraham left, Asad asked me if I had decided if I would allow his tribe to settle near our spring.

"I have been lonely here. Ishmael and I are happy and grateful you have decided to stay."

Asad gestured toward the spring, which had enlarged to meet the needs of so many animals and people. "We have water here, enough we should be able to plant some grains. Herds of animals pass in the other valleys, so we can get meat."

I nodded. We had not hungered since Ishmael had learned to kill the passing herd animals.

"Besides," Asad added, "Abraham requested we stay with you. Ishmael cannot protect you by himself if another tribe should come and try to take the water by force."

I set my hand against my chest. "I would give them water, as I gave it to you. There would be no need for force."

Asad set a hand on my arm. "Unless they want more than the water."

I gasped. "You mean —"

He nodded. "Not all men are good men. You were blessed to have us find you first."

I bowed my head and offered a silent prayer of thanks to Jehovah. When I finished, I asked, "Will your tribe be happy here with us?"

"We took a vote. Everyone agreed this is a good place to settle."

Many of the women became my friends. We gossiped together at the edge of the spring as I had gossiped near the well in Memphis. Sometimes I heard the roaring of an animal in the next valley that reminded me of the crocodile in the Aur as it flowed through Memphis. It always caused me to shudder and remember my brother.

"Why do you shudder when the lions roar in the next valley?" Zulfa asked one day.

"They remind me of the crocodiles in the Aur."

She bent her head. "Many people had terrible experiences with Grandfather Crocodile."

"Is he still alive?" I asked. "I thought he would have died long ago."

"Perhaps the crocodile you knew as Grandfather Crocodile did. But there is an enormous crocodile who roams the edges of the river, seeking tasty bites of Egyptian men, women, and children."

"It is probably the same vicious crocodile who ate my brother."

The women with me surrounded me in an embrace like I had not received in many years. Between the memory of my brother and the embrace, I fought back tears.

"I lived on the edge of the city of Memphis," Zulfa said. "I heard Grandfather Crocodile bellow often. His sons joined his cries. My blood freezes when I hear the bellows of the animals out in the next valley."

Zulfa and I understood each other.

Her mother taught her to cook, weave, and sew. She cheerfully joined me in the necessary chores. We enjoyed our time together.

Ishmael loved Zulfa deeply. They got along well together. I never heard them argue. If they did, they kept it in their tent and did not share it with the rest of us.

It did not take many weeks for Zulfa to show symptoms of carrying a child. Her stomach revolted sometimes after eating her favorite foods. It did not take long for her stomach to grow big with her child.

About five months after Zulfa married Ishmael, we visited with the other women near the spring.

"I was there when Sarah gave birth to Isaac, but I had no responsibility for helping her. I am concerned what we will do when Zulfa's time comes," I said.

Salwa dipped water into her water jugs. "Have you talked with Huda? She is the midwife and healer for the Jorhom tribe."

"I did not know that," Zulfa said. "I have not often needed a healer."

"Nor have I. Not since you came to stay here," I said.

"Huda is a talented healer. She assists all the women during childbirth."

"We will need her to help," I said.

"It will not be for a time," Zulfa added.

"No," Salwa said, "but she likes to examine her women in the months before their birthing."

After that, Huda visited Zulfa often. I offered my gratitude to Jehovah for bringing Huda to us.

When the time came, Huda helped Zulfa deliver a healthy boy. I joined them, holding Zulfa's hand and wiping her brow. I could do little more. I had no knowledge or training in delivering children.

Ishmael glowed when he came in to see his son and wife. *He will make a good father.* They named the boy Nebajoth.

We loved little Nabajoth. His cheerful gurgle kept us giggling. He was our joy. We all loved him, as did the people of the Jorhom tribe. As he grew, he became a kind, courageous, and loveable boy.

When Nebajoth's sister, Dodi, was born, he loved her as much as we did. She loved him and followed after him as often as we would let her.

My Ishmael had become the wild man the angel had foretold. His love for Zulfa never decreased, but he often went out among the wild animals, seeking food and pelts.

At the age of eight, Nebajoth went hunting with his father. When he returned, his glee overflowed in excited cheers. On the donkey he rode, he had tied behind him an antelope he had killed.

Ishmael taught him to gut and skin the antelope, then butcher and preserve it. Zulfa gave him the first slice of the first roast she cooked. He carried it to me.

"Grandmother," he said. "I want you to have the first slice."

I bit my lip. "Are you certain?" I asked.

He nodded enthusiastically. "Yes, Grandmother. You need the first slice."

He watched as I cut off a bite and ate it. "This is the best antelope I have ever eaten."

He bounced up and down. "I knew it would be good. I watched the antelope eat the best grass."

We all laughed, and Ishmael sliced another piece of roast for Nebajoth.

Zulfa and Ishmael had more children in time. She was blessed that her children came to this earth fairly easily.

After we had been in Paran about fifteen years, news came to us of Abraham's journey to Mount Moriah to offer sacrifice. He had taken Isaac with him. A small group of travelers stopped by our spring for water and spent the night. They spoke of the latest news.

"His servants were concerned, for they had not brought a ram to sacrifice. They feared Abraham would consider offering his son," the leader of the travelers said.

Another picked up the story. "Abraham and Isaac left their servants at the base of Mount Moriah and climbed on up alone. Isaac carried the wood they took with them on his back, much like the lamb they sacrificed would carry the firewood. Abraham's servants feared they would not see Isaac again."

"However," the leader took up the story once more after sipping from his mug of wine, "Isaac returned with Abraham. They spoke of finding a ram caught in a thicket that they used for their sacrifice."

I gazed at Ishmael. He nodded at me, probably thinking of what I thought. If Ishmael had been there in Mamre with Abraham and Sarah, Jehovah may have commanded that the sacrifice be Ishmael rather than Isaac.

"It is amazing that they found a ram," Ishmael said. He handed the jug of wine to the travelers.

"Jehovah always provides," I murmured. *Would He have provided a substitute for my Ishmael if He had commanded Abraham to sacrifice Ishmael rather than Isaac?* I hoped so.

Ishmael and I spoke of it when the travelers left.

"Would you have willingly traveled to Moriah with Abraham, knowing you did not take along a sacrifice?" I asked.

"I do not know," Ishmael answered. "It is good that I do not have to find out. I fear I would not have been as trusting as Isaac. I have always wanted to know, to have some control. Isaac did not have that."

"I thank Jehovah that you were not called on to go with Abraham. Perhaps it is a good thing we were sent from Mamre to Paran," I said. "Jehovah knows you. He knows you may not willingly give yourself as an offering."

Ishmael thrust his chest out. "I may have, if Jehovah asked."

"But the men said Isaac did not know. He had to trust Abraham and Jehovah," I said. "Sarah had to know what was happening. I could not do that. I am not as old as Sarah, but you are my only son. I do not know if I could willingly allow you to go with him. Not for that reason."

After that, we worked to trust each other and Jehovah more. We offered more prayers and remembered to worship each Sabbath Day. Ishmael and I taught Zulfa and the children about Jehovah, hoping Abraham would return long enough to baptize them.

Years later, Abraham returned to visit, bent with age. On that visit, he baptized Zulfa and the children who were old enough to accept Jehovah's love and commandments.

While he was with us, Ishmael asked Abraham to give him the right to bless our family to baptize and perform the marriage rites. Abraham ducked his head and shook it slowly.

"I want to do that and I have asked Jehovah many times for permission to give you this privilege." He peered up at Ishmael. "He will not allow it. You have not received the correct training. It is not time for you to receive this honor. I am sorry."

"Can you ask him again?" Ishmael asked.

"I have asked many times in the last years. Last time, I was told I could not ask again. I am sorry." Tears filled Abraham's eyes. "Perhaps this injunction will be lifted someday, but not today." His gaze moved from Ishmael to me.

"But the angel ..." I said.

"He saved you twice. He promised Ishmael would be the father of a great nation." His gaze returned to Ishmael and Zulfa. "Look at your children. Your posterity is growing. Jehovah loves you. But, for now, you may not have this right."

Abraham gathered us into his arms and cried with us. "I will return to provide these rites for your family as often as I can. I will ask Isaac to come bless your lives."

"Isaac," Ishmael exploded. He scattered the remnants of the carving he had been working on. "Always Isaac! You have preferred him to me in everything you do. I am your oldest son. I should inherit your property and the priesthood. But you sent me away so you could give it to Isaac, my younger brother."

"Ishmael," Abraham cried. "It is not that way."

"No?" Ishmael's voice rose. "There was no reason for me to be sent away. I would never hurt Isaac."

"We could not be certain of that. Your anger had become more than I could handle. You refused to obey. What could I do?"

"You could have spent more time with me. All I wanted was to be with you. I wanted you to see me as your son. Not just Isaac." Pain filled Ishmael's voice.

"I tried. But I am old. You went with the herders. They taught you to be independent and to care for the sheep. Look. You have herds of sheep here in a place no one expected to find them."

"No thanks to you," Ishmael spat.

"I sent them to you. I asked Asad to bring them to you." Abraham's voice broke with the pain.

Ishmael shuffled back a step. "Asad said he bought them for me."

"As I asked him. I wanted you to be independent. You could not depend on me. I live too far from you."

Ishmael stomped away from the fire.

Abraham looked at me and lifted his eyebrows. "What more can I say? Jehovah refuses."

"That is all you can say. We must continue to follow Him without those blessings. It will be difficult ..."

"But you can do it, if you teach your grandchildren well."

"She taught me," Zulfa said from the other side of the fire.

Abraham took the youngest from her and held her in his lap. "I believe the mothers of our families will be the ones to teach our children. Fathers work hard and cannot always be there to teach the children. We depend on you."

"I have worked to teach Ishmael and all my grandchildren," I said.

Abraham turned to me, bouncing the baby on his knee. "It shows. Look at your posterity, our posterity."

"I will do my best to keep teaching them."

Abraham continued to love me, although he did not invite me or Ishmael to return to Mamre. Our lives had separated. We would never be close as we were before Ishmael's birth again. It was as though the crocodiles had invaded my life once more.

Acknowledgements

Another book written, and you stayed with me to read it!

I give thanks to my readers who asked me to write this series. I didn't want to write the stories of the wives and concubines of Abraham, Isaac, and Jacob. How can I compete with those others who have written of some of these women? But, since my readers requested it, I am writing them — all seven books!

First and foremost, I must thank my patient sweetheart, Jack, for his constant support. Some days I sit at my desk, others I sit beside him in front of the television, ignoring him as I am lost in my stories. Without his support, I would never have written any books.

My family always supports me, including all my children and grandchildren, and my parents. I am grateful for their support. My mom and dad do all they can to help, and my dad, who is now 95, is my final proofreader! Without their support, it would be much more difficult to write.

I thank my friends and members of American Night Writers Association (ANWA) who have supported me and helped me write in daily sprinting groups. Because we write as fast as possible for 30 minutes at a time, much of this book has been written. Thanks especially go to Carol Malone.

As always, this book would not be as good of a story without the efforts of my editor, Julia Allen. With her careful editing, this book is more readable and enjoyable for you to read. Additionally, the amazing skills of my cover artist, Dar Albert, have come through in this beautiful cover. Both ladies deserve my heartfelt thanks.

Many thanks to my AngelCAST team, who have read the final version and found the last typos and mistakes. Thank you, team!

Last, but never least, a big thank you goes to you, my reader, for choosing to read this book of fiction I spent my time writing. I would love to hear how you liked it, or if you have suggestions. Email me at Angelique@AngeliqueCongerAuthor.com.

Also By Angelique Conger

Ancient Matriarchs
Eve, First Matriarch
Into the Storms: Ganet, Wife of Seth
Finding Peace: Rebecca, Wife of Enos
Moving into Light: Zehira, Wife of Enoch
Out of Darkness: Imma, Wife of Noah
We Stood with Them: Other Wives of the Prophets
Lost Children of the Prophet
Lost Children of the Prophet
Captured Freedom
Abandoned Hope
Brotherly Havoc
Betrayed Trust
Convicted Deliverance
Trouble Escaped
Contrary Devotion
Impassioned Grief
Love Defied
Hidden Purpose
Concealed Innocence
Struggle for Limhah
Combating Cults
Fighting Foreign Armies
Defending Faith
Into Egypt

HAGAR, MOTHER OF SORROWS

Before Egypt
Discovery
Settlement
Enemies
Women of the Covenant
Sarah, Mother of Nations
Hagar, Mother of Sorrows
Rebekah, Mother of Hope

About the Author

Many would consider Angelique Conger's books Christian focused, and they are because they focus on early events in the Bible. She writes of a people's beliefs in Jehovah. However, though she's read in much of the Bible and searched for more about these stories, there isn't much there. Her imagination fills in the missing information, which is most of it.

Angelique Conger discovered the wonders of writing books later in her life. Books, however, have always been important to her. As a little girl in a small town, she was given her own library card at the tender age of five, highly unusual in those days.

Angelique reads a book, or three at once, much of the time. She reads most genres of books and, until a few years ago, only toyed with writing them. Since beginning, she has spent many hours each day learning the craft of writing and editing.

Angelique lives in Southern Nevada with her husband, Siamese cat, Sparky, and their tuxedo cat, Spicy. She enjoys visits from her grandchildren and their parents.

Don't miss out!

Visit the website below and you can sign up to receive emails whenever Angelique Conger publishes a new book. There's no charge and no obligation.

https://books2read.com/r/B-A-NFPH-VCGPC

BOOKS 2 READ

Connecting independent readers to independent writers.